MW00463319

Moon Over

Laramie

VIVIAN SINCLAIR

DISCARD

Copyright

Published by East Hill Books

This book is a work of fiction. Names, characters, and incidents either are the product of the author's imagination or are used fictitiously. Any resemblance to actual persons, living or dead, or events is entirely coincidental.

Copyright © 2015, 1st edition, by Vivian Sinclair Books.

All rights reserved.

Cover design: © Vivian Sinclair Books

Cover illustrations credit:

Thuatha22 | Dreamstime.com

Denis Belitskiy | Dreamstime.com

ISBN-13: 978-1522847083

ISBN-10: 1522847081

Books by Vivian Sinclair available in print or Kindle at Amazon.com:

A Guest At The Ranch, western contemporary romance

Storm In A Glass Of Water, a small town story

A Walk In The Rain, women's fiction novel

The Maitland Legacy, western contemporary romance series:

    Book 1 – ***Lost In Wyoming*** – Lance's story

    Book 2 – ***Moon Over Laramie*** – Tristan's story

    Book 3 – ***Christmas In Cheyenne*** – Raul's story

To find out about new releases and about other books written by Vivian Sinclair visit her website at www.viviansinclairbooks.com

PROLOGUE

It was a warm summer night. The sky was reddish to the west where the sun had set beyond the horizon and dark above, with twinkling stars in an astronomer's delight. A glorious full moon was reigning over the Laramie plains.

Tristan and his nine year old son Zach were rocking in two identical chairs on the porch of their newly bought house on the outskirts of Laramie, Wyoming.

Tristan had despaired that the realtor would not be able to find a house to suit them. Some, closer to downtown, were too small, with minuscule backyards. Others were too far in the country for a convenient commute. When the realtor had called Tristan to tell him a new property just came on the market, he had been skeptical. But as soon as he saw the house, he knew it was perfect for him and Zach. It was a sprawling ranch house on over forty acres of land, close to his veterinarian practice. There were two outbuildings, one a large shop, the other a barn with stalls for their increasing menagerie of animals. His son was collecting stray animals like other kids collected toys. They had two horses, three dogs, two cats, and a baby goat. The goat had been a gift for Zach from his uncle Lance and it was white and cute.

"Dad," Zach said in a small voice. "Do you think Mama can see this moon?"

Tristan was stunned. It had been several years since Zach had asked about his mother. He was a very well-adjusted boy, easy-going, liked by his friends and classmates.

Before Tristan could answer, Zach continued, "Sometimes when I look at the moon, I think maybe Mama is looking at it too. And we could meet like this…. "

His son was yearning for a mother figure. What could Tristan say to this? Zach's mother had been young, ready to enjoy life and had no desire to be saddled with a kid. As soon as Zach was born, she signed away her parental rights and left never to be heard of again. Tristan assumed all the responsibility of raising Zach, trying his best to be both father and mother. He excelled in guiding Zach at homework and in sports and burned most of his attempts to bake cookies, but all in all they managed pretty well together. Zach was the light of his life, and his reason for getting up in the morning.

Tristan had been a lone wolf all his life. As a little boy, just adopted by Elliott Maitland, he thought he'd have a family. But his adoptive father was a busy man and uninterested to spend time with him. He tried to be friends with his older brothers, but they were six years older and ignored him most of the time. His attempts to get their attention ended tragically when his brother Lance broke his leg in three places and almost lost his leg.

Rejected by everybody, he grew up a loner, keeping company with the animals. With them he had a special bond and they accepted him easily. His decision to become a veterinarian came naturally. Now his dream was fulfilled.

Recently being accepted by his brothers was a bonus and he had his future sister-in-law, Annie to thank for that.

His motherless son Zach loved animals as much as Tristan did and he was a happy nine-year old boy. Or so Tristan thought.

CHAPTER 1

The wedding between Lance Maitland, local rancher and son of one of the wealthiest men in southeastern Wyoming and Annabelle Lacroix, writer from New York City was THE event of the summer, creating so much buzz that all the locals invited were happy to accept, forsaking other plans. Usually in July the main attraction was the Cheyenne Frontier Days and rodeo. Many ranch hands were competing in the rodeo and the friends and families were going to Cheyenne to support them and attend the rodeo. Ranchers in the area supplied the livestock necessary for the competitions, wild mustangs, bulls for riding, steers and calves for the roping and wrestling contests.

This summer though, the Maitland wedding was generating more interest than the Frontier Days. The story of how a local boy swept the New Yorker off her feet and after a whirlwind courtship proposed to her and how the old man Maitland spared no expense to make this a dream wedding, spread all over this corner of Wyoming.

The affair was planned on a grand scale, although the groom and the bride had wanted a smaller party with only friends and family. They had been overruled by the father of the groom, Maitland himself and the mother of the bride, Mrs. Jackson, who were getting along famously in organizing the wedding.

The backyard of the ranch house was flooded with hundreds of flowers, brought by the florist in special coolers from far away parts of the country. Not many flowers grew in the rocky soil and harsh climate of Wyoming, although Annie, the bride, swore she would have a little garden behind their ranch house and give it all the care that was needed to make her plants grow.

"Mama, these shoes pinch my toes," Annie complained, wriggling her toes out of the Jimmy Choo white sandals that her mother had reverently taken out of their box.

"They are supposed to make your feet look smaller," her mother said, adjusting Annie's veil over her wildly curled hair, tamed in a topknot with tendrils artfully arranged around her face. Not even a lot of spray had succeeded to restrain the curls and more and more of them were escaping the knot.

"What does it matter if her feet look small or not? Nobody will see them. She wears a long gown," Eleanor, the younger sister argued.

"At least she can wear elegant high-heels. Her groom is as tall as a bear." The older sister, Lauren was married to a distinguished thoracic surgeon, who was a little on the short side and she had to wear flats all the time.

Ignoring Lauren, their mother threw a fulminating look at her youngest daughter. "Eleanor, you have no business interfering. Annie's dress is longer because it was supposed to be yours and you are much taller than she is. The dressmaker in New York did her best to alter it, but with the time so short and Annie unwilling to come back even for one day, this is the best she could do." She wiped an imaginary tear, careful not to blot her mascara. "By now you should have been married to dear James. But no, you had to antagonize all the influential people in New York City, to jeopardize your career and break up with James right before your wedding."

"Mama, we've been through this before," Eleanor said using her tough prosecutor's voice. "I don't want James. I'm sorry you had to cancel all the plans and invitations, but I covered all the expenses."

"Ellie should marry for love," Annie, the bride chimed in.

Her mother admonished her, shaking her finger. "Annie, you are now scatterbrained because you are in love. You are lucky that Lance is not as poor as we all believed. For Eleanor, James was perfect."

"He was not if she didn't love him," Annie continued to argue, although when her mother's mind was set, it was pointless to try to convince her otherwise.

8

"All right girls, let's go," the mother said after she inspected them all. "And Annie, be careful not to trip over the dress."

Advancing with Lauren through rows of chairs and hundreds of invitees to the makeshift altar under a recently built arbor, Eleanor was considering her mother's words. She did not doubt her decisions, life-altering as they were. She didn't want 'dear James' for a husband, rich and handsome as he was. He had proved himself to be self-centered and shallow. Besides, James was presently embroiled in an affair with another woman and not thinking of marriage. She was sure also that her dream to be a judge in New York City was not what she wanted now. She was confused as to what to do with her life. She had a law degree and a good brain. If only she knew what she wanted, she reflected, taking her place as bridesmaid together with Lauren at the left of the altar.

To the right, the groom, Lance Maitland and his two brothers and best men, Tristan and Raul were waiting for the bride to come. Annie and her mother descended slowly the few stairs of the back porch.

Eleanor heard Lance saying in awe, "She is so beautiful."

She looked at Annie, pretty in her designer dress, a bit tottering on the high-heeled Jimmy Choo's. Her curls were springing merrily from the pins and from the veil, unaffected by the ton of hair spray in which Mama had bathed them. Annie was slowly advancing toward her groom, radiantly smiling at him with love in her eyes. It was then that Eleanor knew. She wanted what Annie had found in this most unexpected way and place. She wanted a man to love her, to find the one and only for her. She wanted the happiness that shone in Annie's eyes. As for her career, she was smart and could pass the bar exam in any state and work as a lawyer anywhere.

The wedding vows were said. The ring, carried by Zach, was placed on Annie's finger, and the pair was pronounced man and wife by the pastor. The bride was kissed and wild shouts of 'Ye-haa' erupted all over the place. The invitees were overly-enthusiastic.

The music started, the feast on the tables was impressive, and many toasted the newly-wed couple.

There were some New Yorkers invited who were none too shy to try a country dance or toast together with the locals one glass of drink too many. Eleanor was supposed to keep company with Patrick Finnegan, the son of her mother's best friend, Bitsy.

Eleanor knew she was beautiful, tall, slim, with natural blond hair and blue eyes, and with pure, regular features. It was a blessing and a curse. Some people assumed she was a decorative, featherbrained blonde. Clichéd, but it happened. They were surprised to realize how smart she was, while others were downright disappointed not to be able to condescendingly say, 'Don't bother your pretty head'. She learned early on to keep her thoughts and feelings to herself, hidden under an impassive, serene mask. It had been especially useful in her career as prosecutor. Men had labeled her 'the ice queen'. It was an irony, considering that she was very emotional and temperamental in reality.

"I think you feel as out of place in this … country environment as I feel," a voice whispered in her ear brushing wet lips on her sensitive skin.

Tempering her instinctive reaction to wipe her ear, Eleanor answered without turning, "Actually, Patrick, I'm enjoying my sister's wedding. People are genuinely happy and having fun. I've attended so many weddings and parties back east, where it was all pretend, all about social status and making a grand impression on the others." She smiled at Annie's blissfully happy face, in the arms of her tall, blond cowboy, both moving slowly in a rhythm all of their own in the middle of the rowdy, twirling and whistling dancers.

Eleanor's eyes glanced over her sister and her groom to the dark, brooding figure, standing at the edge of the makeshift party space, watching the dancers with unfathomable dark eyes.

Following her look, Patrick sneered at her. "Don't tell me you share your sister's taste for unpolished, uneducated country bumpkins? I mean Annie has always been a bit strange, with romantic, unrealistic ideas, but you, Eleanor were considered the epitome of beauty and refinement."

The insult to her sister was enough to spring a harsh rebuke to her lips, but she remembered that Patrick was not the brightest mind even when he was sober. Unfortunately, he was rarely sober, his penchant for drinking being notorious among their friends.

"If you are referring to the brother of the groom, then I don't know him well, but your prejudice is off the mark in his case. He is a veterinarian doctor. Do the math. He has more years of education than you and I."

Patrick shook his head as if to chase away the alcohol fumes clouding his thinking. Finally he said, "You know Eleanor, when I heard that James had called off the wedding I thought you might have melted a little and I hoped that you would give the rest of us decent men, a chance. Only it didn't happen. You are the same snotty ice-queen who doesn't know how to be nice when a guy approaches her."

Eleanor had enough of his drunken ramblings and she turned to tell him so, when little Zach grabbed her hand to get her attention. "Ellie, my dog Toro was supposed to stay in the barn during the wedding, but he's not there. You have to help me find him."

Annoyed by this interference, Patrick snapped at him, "Beat it, boy. Can't you see we are talking?"

Eleanor winked at Zach and muttering an 'Excuse me' to Patrick turned her back on him and followed Zach to the barn.

"Well Zach, where was Toro when you last saw him?" she asked.

Zach seemed inordinately interested in the straws on the barn's floor, shuffling his feet. "It's not

Toro. How could he be lost? If I whistle he'll come to me immediately." To prove his point, he did just that and the puppy came yapping right away. Wiggling his tail he stopped in front of the boy and looked at him expectantly. Zach picked him up praising him. "Good boy, Toro."

Eleanor laughed. "How silly of me! Of course he was not lost. Then what happened, Zach?"

He looked at her, with dark eyes shadowed by long, curled eyelashes, so like his father's and sighed. "I thought to talk to you because you are so smart, and know what to do."

At least this was one male person who admired her intelligence. "Yes, Zach you can talk to me," she answered.

"First you have to promise not to tell a soul what I'm about to tell you."

It could have been only a child's natural inclination to secrecy and conspiracy, but it could also be serious. Eleanor was a district attorney and had seen too many cases to take this so-called confession easily. "What I can promise is to consider your problem seriously and if it's not dangerous to solve it between us. If it is important or threatening in any way, then your father needs to be informed."

A few moments of silence followed as Zach thought this through. Finally he nodded. "Okay. It's like this. A week ago, when the summer basketball camp was over and I was waiting for my ride, a lady approached me and told me she was my mother and it was time we two met and got to know each other."

Eleanor was stunned. "I thought your mother had died when you were born."

Zach shook his head. "No, she didn't die. She just left after I was born. Dad told me she was too young and afraid to be responsible for a kid. But Dad was the same age and afraid or not, he took the responsibility to raise me alone. It must have been me she didn't want."

"No Zach." Eleanor bent down to be at eye level with him. "Whatever the truth is, I am sure that any parent, young or not would be happy to have you as a child. I can assure you of this much, that whatever problems she had then were all of her own."

CHAPTER 2

"You know Ellie, so many times I thought of my mother, of what she looks like, how she talks or smiles. This woman was so different, so far from what I imagined…" Zach sighed again.

Oh, the mess adults make, careless of how they hurt the kids they are supposed to protect, Eleanor thought. "In what way, Zach?"

"I had this fantasy, you see, that my mother will come back and tell me she's sorry she left me, but that she loves me." He looked at Eleanor with eyes full of tears. "I guess it was just a fantasy because this woman was nothing like this. She looked around with shifting eyes, as if worried someone would catch her talking to me. One thing for sure was that she was not sorry for leaving and staying away. This woman was not concerned about me. It was like… she had to do this, talk to me and such." He sniffed. "You see what I mean, Ellie?"

What Eleanor saw was a potentially

dangerous situation and Tristan had to be informed about it as soon as possible. "Listen Zach, this woman might not even be your mother…"

"She was," Zach confirmed. "She said her name was Norah Sanders. This is the name on my birth certificate and she showed me a picture of herself with my father ten years ago, the year before I was born."

"Even if she is your birth mother, until we know exactly what she wants, you have to stay away from her if she comes back."

Zach interrupted. "She did. Next day. She wanted me to go with her to get to know each other…"

Fear speared Eleanor. She grabbed his arms, pulling him to her. "Oh Zach, I hope you didn't…"

"Nah, she didn't seem very interested to know me and that day after camp Jake - that's my best friend - and I, we agreed to play some soccer at the field. Jake came to see why I was late." He caressed Eleanor's cheek. "Don't worry Ellie. I wouldn't have gone with her. Dad has drilled me many times about not going anywhere with strangers. Although I would have liked to get to know her better," he added wistfully.

She had to make him understand the dangers in this situation. Eleanor took a deep breath. "You have to trust me in this, Zach. This woman does not have the legal right to decide where you go and with whom. Only your father does. Not only because he raised you since birth, but because the law says so. There are a lot of dangers and deviant, abusive people and the law, in order to protect innocent little kids from such people, decides who will take care of the kid. In this case, your father. I'm sorry if my decision disappoints you, I understand you wanted to know your mother, but without your father's knowledge and approval I don't think it is right. We have to tell him."

The little dog, bored, started running around their legs. Zach picked him up. "I know. It's just that whenever I ask about Mama he gets upset and he gets these grooves near his mouth like when he is really sad and has this faraway look. I don't want to upset him."

She ruffled his dark hair. "He will be more upset if you don't tell him. Besides, you have to make your father aware of what's going on and to trust that he is the best person to deal with this situation." Zach nodded in agreement. "Let's go find him and tell him now."

Outside, the wedding party was still in full swing and after so much toasting the newlyweds the guests were even more merry. The bride and groom had disappeared and Raul was trying to convince his father to take a rest and Eleanor's mother was galloping around the dance ring in the arms of a white-haired, but vigorous rancher. The New Yorkers had blended well with the locals and held their own in both dancing and toasting. Bitsy Finnegan was laughing at whatever the mustachioed cowboy near her was saying, while Patrick, in the nostalgic phase of wine imbibing was slouched in a chair ogling the ample décolletage of a local beauty, who was laughing and slapping half-heartedly at his roaming hand.

On the opposite side of the garden, Tristan was looking for Zach and meeting their eyes across the party space, he came to them at once. Holding Zach's hand, Eleanor marched back to the barn for more privacy.

"All right, what have Zach … or his puppy done?" Tristan added looking at the playful little dog which was jumping around.

"Ah Dad, why do you assume I did something wrong?" Zach protested.

"He didn't," Eleanor interjected. "I'll let him explain what happened."

Worried now, Tristan turned his attention to his son. "What is going on, Zach?"

Zach gulped and looking at his father blurted. "Mama came to see me a week ago after summer camp."

"What?" Tristan exploded, not sure he heard

right.

Eleanor touched his arm. "Calm down, Tristan. Zach is confused, scared, and torn between his desire to get to know his mother, which is natural, and not wanting to upset you. This woman came to see him after practice hours and approached Zach telling him her name is Norah Sanders and showing him a picture of the two of you from ten years ago."

Tristan raked his short hair with his fingers. "Why now? Why didn't you tell me right away?" he asked Zach.

Eleanor placed her hand protectively on Zach's shoulder. "Because he didn't want to upset you. There is more. The next day, she came again and tried to coax Zach to climb into her car for a drive. He didn't go and she left."

"She said she'll be back," Zach said in a small voice.

Eleanor looked at Tristan. "I have to ask you, do you have full custody?" Tristan hesitated and Eleanor was sorry for interfering. "Look, if you want me to butt out, I will. It's a very private, personal matter…"

"No, no. Lord knows what might have happened if you had not told me."

Zach looked down at his overly energetic dog. "I'm sorry I didn't tell you, Dad. It was wrong of me."

Tristan pulled Zach to him. "You're my life Zach. We'll get through this together." Then he addressed Eleanor. "To answer your question, Yes, I have full custody. We were both nineteen when we met, freshmen at University of Colorado in Denver. She was pretty, from a wealthy family and had no plans for the future except to have fun in college. When we realized she was pregnant, she informed me in no uncertain terms that she was too young to have a kid. I convinced her to leave Zach to me. The day he was born, she signed away her parental rights, went away, and never looked back. I never heard from her again." He covered his face with his hands. "Why now? She must have some interest of some sort. But what? I'm not rich for her to ask me for money."

"She sure didn't care to get to know me better, although so she claimed," Zach observed, disappointment in his voice.

"Could she be desperate and try to force him to come with her?" Tristan wondered. "Zach is involved in a lot of activities, sports mostly, basketball, soccer, when he is not riding. He is also doing a special science project together with his friend Jake. Jake's Mom is driving them back and forth to all these summer activities, but she has seven kids and is frazzled by all the work. I can't ask her to pay special attention to Zach or to be with the boys all the time. I will have to drive him there myself and pick him up when the classes are over," he mused aloud, trying to figure out a way to leave his busy practice at all odd hours. "I would hate to curtail all his summer activities and fun. It would be unfair."

"I can do that for you if you trust me," Eleanor offered. "I mean Annie and Lance will go honeymooning in the Florida Keys for two weeks and I thought of returning to New York City for lack of a better alternative. Exploring Laramie and riding horses is rather tempting until I decide what to do." All of a sudden this idea held more appeal to her than returning to New York. "I'll bring Zach to the clinic after his sports hours."

Tristan was surprised by her offer. After the passionate kiss they shared the night the rustlers had been caught, Eleanor had kept her distance, letting him know in an unspoken way that the kiss was a mistake she didn't care to repeat. He got the message loud and clear and didn't come closer. He had plenty of problems of his own and they were piling up daily. "Well, of course I trust you. But this is my problem. I don't want to inconvenience you."

She waved her hand dismissing the argument. "You don't. After all I am your sister-in-law of sorts." In fact, Tristan was not blood related to Lance. He had been adopted by Maitland when he was four years old and so they became brothers.

Zach, who had been following the conversation between the two adults, cheered up considerably at this turn of events. "Ellie could come to live with us. We have plenty of space."

"Eleanor might have other plans," Tristan replied.

"I don't want to be in the way..." Eleanor protested. She didn't, but then where would she stay? At Annie and Lance's ranch, except that they were in the Florida Keys and it didn't make much sense to drive all the way from the ranch to town only to watch over Zach during summer activities. She could stay at a hotel in Laramie, but they might not accept her little dog, Cleo.

"We have plenty of space and you will love our place. Just wait until you see all our animals. You'll love them." Zach tried to convince her.

"There really is a lot of space and in fact it will be only for a short time until I succeed to talk to Zach's birth mother and figure out what she wants," Tristan said.

The truth was that this was the best solution and the most convenient for all involved. It gave Eleanor a little more time to figure out what to do with the rest of her life. Besides, it tempted her to be here when Annie would return from her honeymoon. At present it looked like the zany sister had succeeded the best of all three sisters in finding the key to happiness in life.

"All right, guys, we got a deal," she heard herself saying.

CHAPTER 3

After Katherine Maitland, second wife of the family patriarch Elliott Maitland, Tristan's mother, moved to Denver, the big ranch house became more inviting and cheerful. Gone were the dark, heavy velvet drapes that covered the windows. The house was full of light, sparkling clean, and colorful pillows and flowers brightened every room.

Raul took his father to see a cardiologist in Cheyenne and after being poked and prodded and tested, the old man was assured he would live many more years if he ate a healthy diet and took his medications regularly. Raul brought him back to the ranch to be able to watch over his health.

Carmelita, Raul's mother, moved to the big ranch house and took over the cooking and taking care of the house. Because Raul liked to eat together with his men, the large table in the kitchen became a gathering place at breakfast and dinner for all the cowboys. No more bunkhouse meals for them or having to eat Pepe's cooking.

The transition in the cattle business management had been surprisingly smooth, although Raul's style was very different than the old man's. While his father liked to bark orders at everyone, Raul listened to the men before making a decision then quietly saw things done exactly as he wanted. He was not the hothead the men feared he would be. On the contrary, he was pretty amiable. However, his authority was undeniable and he earned the well-deserved respect of all the ranch hands. Old Man Maitland kept his promise not to interfere. Although he was mumbling and grumbling daily, in reality he was pleased that his ranch was in good hands and that Raul had proven to be such a capable leader.

Lucky was promoted to foreman and as such he carried himself with dignity claiming that the pranks of the past were... of the past, because he was now a man with responsibility.

The day after the wedding, breakfast was a late affair as people were nursing various degrees of headache related to the intensity of toasting the newly-wed couple.

Eleanor watched her mother daintily placing a linen napkin in her lap. Where did she find a linen napkin? Eating in the kitchen was rather informal and the napkins were plain paper. The older cowboy near her was explaining about cattle stomach colic and her mother was nodding as if cattle colic was the most important thing in her life. To give her mother her due, she had made Annie proud on her wedding day. She had talked and laughed and danced with all the cowboys, be they simple ranch hands or wealthy ranchers, making them all feel important and welcomed guests.

The back door opened and Tristan came in bringing with him a rush of fresh cool morning air from outside. He deposited a kiss on Carmelita's cheek, whispering that he could not start the day without her pancakes. Unlike the day before when he had been dressed in a very elegant charcoal suit, today he had on jeans, a flannel plaid shirt, and a denim jacket. He looked at Eleanor and his dark eyes warmed as her pulse responded by accelerating. If he could create such havoc on her senses with only one look, then a touch would be an electric shock. Their mutual physical attraction might be a problem, not that Eleanor was adverse to see where this might lead, but she wanted much more than this. She wanted what Annie had. That deep, profound love when you feel the other one is as necessary to your life as the air to breathe.

"Where is Zach?" she asked him, looking at the platter full of warm pancakes Carmelita was placing on the table rather than meeting his eyes.

Tristan laughed. "In the barn, assisting Raul with a newborn calf. I hope this doesn't mean we'll increase our own livestock. There are plenty now and I barely manage to take care of them all before going to work." But his smile belied his words because he loved all animals.

Eleanor's mother finished with breakfast and exhausting all the aspects of cattle colic with her table neighbor, took her plate to the sink and rinsed it. "Eleanor, will you come upstairs, please?"

Eleanor looked at Tristan and said in a low voice, "I'm packed and ready to go. I'll see what Mama wants and be back."

In her room, her mother was also ready packed and debating in front of the mirror between a blue scarf to match her eyes or a green one to match her silk blouse. "I hope you're ready, Eleanor. Dear Brandon will be here to pick us up in half an hour."

Eleanor crossed her arms. "Dear Brandon?" she inquired smiling.

Her mother finally decided for the blue scarf, knotted it loosely around her neck, and nodded with satisfaction. "Yes. Brandon is a distinguished rancher from around here. He offered to teach me to ride, you know. Not at my age, I answered. But he replied that from what he can see, I seem to have a very good seat."

Eleanor masked her laugh with an artful cough.

"Now, are you ready to go? He'll drive us to Denver, which is a blessing because I don't want to fly ever again in that small commuter plane from Denver to Laramie. It was such a bumpy flight, and the plane so tiny and old, right out of Charles Lindbergh's times. Dear Brandon will arrange to have the rental car delivered back to the office in Laramie."

"Mama, I…" Eleanor started to say.

"What?"

"I'm not going," she blurted. "Not yet."

"What do you mean you're not going? You're expected in New York City to pursue your career goal to be a judge, and perhaps to mend the broken relationship with James." Her mother plopped down on the bed near her open, full suitcase.

"Mama, you are not listening. There is nothing to mend. I don't want James."

Her mother waved her hand. "Oh, I listen, I do. Even if I don't like what I'm hearing. Annie and Lance are in Florida. So what are you going to do here? You said you had no interest in the Raul person. So why are you staying here?"

"I'm not exactly going to stay here?" she mumbled.

Her mother should have been a prosecutor. She was so determined in her interrogation. She looked straight at Eleanor. "Then where are you...?" She covered her mouth with her hand. "Dear Lord, don't tell me it's the vet you're after? I mean, he's handsome in a dark, brooding way, I'll give you that. But he's poor and he's not even part of the family. He was adopted. Not to mention his disgraced mother, who ran away to Denver. I don't know the story here, but Elliott Maitland and she are separated. I wouldn't be surprised if he divorced her."

"Mama, first, these are rumors that have nothing to do with Tristan. Second, I don't know him very well. I like him, but it's too early to speculate what the future might bring."

"This is the problem with you girls. You squander your precious years of youth on men you are not even sure you like." When Eleanor opened her mouth to protest, she raised her hand. "Yes, it is like this. Look at Annie and Ed, and you and James. Why can't you make up your mind what you want and go after it?"

"Oh, Mama." Eleanor embraced her mother. "I will. I promise. I just need to stay a little longer here. I don't want to return to New York City right now, to the old routine, the same people, and the same life. I need the distance to put things in perspective. I'll be fine, you'll see."

"Just don't take too long. You are younger than Annie, but not by much." Sighing, her mother closed her suitcase and kissing Eleanor, she left the room.

In the past, it was called the parlor and today the living-room, not very much used regardless of the name, the Old Man thought looking around. He was sitting in a comfortable recliner, with a book and some papers on his lap, and a cup of tea on the round table nearby. Looking at Tristan who had just entered the room to say hello, he said emphatically, "I feel useless."

Tristan seated himself in the opposite chair and considered the old man's predicament. "You know you can't work on the range like you did before. Raul is doing a good job taking care of the ranch..."

"No, no." The Old Man shook his head. "I promised I would not interfere with his decisions and I will not. Besides the doctor has forbidden it. On the other hand, I ain't dead yet, so what am I to do with myself? I feel like a horse who is too old to run, but not old enough to be put out to pasture."

Tristan understood very well that for such an active man his father needed to feel useful. He was bored. "I don't think Raul would agree to your initial intention to move to Cheyenne. Be realistic! You need Carmelita's good food and care and to remind you to take your medications. But I understand you being bored. Let me talk to Lance and Raul and see what we can come up with…." Tristan hesitated before finally deciding to ask what was on his mind. "Do you miss Mama?"

The old man narrowed his eyes. "I didn't know she had an affair with Warner right under my nose. This makes me an old fool. But I miss her wit, the challenge to live with her every day and yes, the sex. I know you young people think I'm too decrepit to think of sex."

Tristan didn't need to hear about his parents' sex life. "For what it's worth, I'm sorry she cheated on you…."

"I didn't love her, boy. Women attach great importance to being loved. I didn't. I couldn't. I was still mourning my first wife. Katherine didn't love me either. We had an understanding, but she would have liked to be adored and to be able to rule around here. I didn't make either possible for her."

"Are you going to divorce her?"

"Do you think I should?"

Tristan nodded. "Yes, I think you should. I

can't imagine being married to a woman who cheated on me."

Maitland took a sip of the tea, looked through the window at the wide open space that was his ranch and said in a barely audible voice, "All these years we lived together your mother had a personal bank account where she periodically increased the balance. I knew to the cent how much she had and she gathered a tidy sum there. Unfortunately for her she paid a big chunk to bail out that no good Cole Warner and he ran away. He was caught in Texas, but the bail money was forfeit. When her money runs out, she'll be back. She will not live in a house where Raul is master, but she'll try to get more money. I'm telling you this so you'll be aware that she had a lot of money when she left me. Oh, she'll ask you for money too. To be sure."

Tristan opened his hands in exasperation. "What can I do Old Man? She's my mother."

Maitland coughed. "For starters, you could try calling me Father. Raul does. Lance did before, and he'll come around. The skinny New Yorker he married will make him. She's   big into this family idea."

"And you are not?" Tristan smiled. "Why don't you admit you loved to play the family patriarch at the wedding?"

"The family patriarch? Hmm…"

"Very well, Father." Tristan conceded, trying out this new word on his tongue.   "What? You don't have to, if you don't want to." The old man amended. Maybe it was too late to heal the wounds of a lifetime.

"No, no. I like calling you Father. It's just that I have often wondered. You knew my mother before I was born…"

"I'm not your father. I wish I were, but the truth is I'm not."

"I know that." Tristan raised his hand to placate him. Then he spoke slowly, hesitating. "I just wondered maybe you knew who he was. My biological father."

The old man was surprised by the question. "No, I don't. For sure, only Katherine knows. I know she was young, beautiful, and had many admirers. Let me think about it and to the best of my recollection I'll tell you which one of them seemed more probable. I could tell you to ask her, but I doubt she'll tell you, unless you pay her and if she wants money badly, then she might."

Maitland knew well Tristan's mother's mercenary and greedy nature.

"I couldn't pay her even if I wanted. I just bought a house for Zach and I. By the way, I hope you'll come to visit us. Thank you for this conversation. It's more than we ever had all these years."

He bent and kissed the old man's cheek. "Good bye, Father."

CHAPTER 4

"Tristan," the Old Man called him back from the door. "There were three men your mother was keeping company with. This is to the best of my recollection after more than thirty years have gone by. The one she liked best was a charming rogue, called Walter Dunn. He was flamboyant, enjoyed partying a lot, and treated your mother like a princess. He had no job other than gambling. He was always ready for a game of cards, and most times he won. Some people said he was cheating. Possible, but he was never caught. When he had money, he was euphoric, ordering drinks for everyone present. Your mother adored him."

Tristan came back and sat in the same chair, facing his father. "Do I look like him?"

The old man pondered this for a while. "Maybe. He was tall, dark, and handsome. But you do resemble your mother very much. I guess anyone of them could be your father."

"What happened to this Walter Dunn?"

"I'm not sure. One day he disappeared and your mother never ever said his name again, as if he had never existed. Did they have a fight and they parted ways? I don't know. I remember several months afterwards, I asked a barman how come Dunn was absent. He said that all he knew was that Dunn had a fight with another guy who hit his head and died, and Dunn was in prison. Is it true? I don't know."

"Great! It is possible my father was a card shark and a cheater and a jailbird," Tristan observed with bitterness.

"His fate and who he was in general has no connection with the decent person that you are. I understand your curiosity to know more about your biological roots, but legally you are my son and practically you are your own man, with your life and success. Whatever you'll discover, remember this and don't let it weigh you down."

"Were all my mother's lovers such lousy

characters?"

"No, not at all. Think about me, I was one of them."

Tristan looked at him surprised. "Yes, well, this is another fact that I don't understand. How come you knew about the others? Didn't she keep them secret?"

"All this happened before you were born. I met her after my first wife died and I came to Cheyenne on and off when I could. Not only did your mother make no secret that she was courted by many men, but also she paraded us one in front of the other. Her price for exclusivity was marriage."

"And you paid this price several years later..."

The Old Man was looking through the window without really seeing, his thoughts lost in a long ago time when he was young and impetuous, thinking Katherine was the answer to what he needed, a beautiful, decorative and smart wife, he was sure he would never love and never suffer like in his first unhappy marriage. "Yes, but I thought of you, too. You were four years old and needed a better environment to grow up in. I thought it would solve all our problems. I'll be honest with you. I was tired of driving all the way to Cheyenne and playing your mother's games only for a night or two in her bed."

Grabbing the teapot, Tristan poured himself a cup of the now tepid tea. "All right, what about the others?"

"The other one was an older man, about forty-five or fifty. I considered him old then. Young buck, I'd say now. He was not from Cheyenne, but visited quite often. He had some interests in a mining consortium from Colorado and traveled a lot all over the western states. He had a lot of money and spent them lavishly on Katherine. Like the other one, one day he ceased coming to town. I don't know what happened to him. When I asked Katherine, she said, 'Who? That old fart? He's gone and good riddance'. All I can tell you is his name, Edgar Hartman. I remember that I thought Edgar such a fuddy-duddy name."

Tristan sighed. "What did he look like?"

"Interestingly enough, he was quite good looking, much more manly than Katherine's preferred one, the gambler. He was tall, with black hair, starting to go grey at his temples and piercing blue eyes. He was a fine figure of a man and I suppose you resemble him a little. Of course you have Katherine's dark eyes."

"Okay, this one was better, although by now he's probably eighty if he's alive. Thank you for telling me. What about the third one?"

"The third one was a Cheyenne resident of about thirty years of age. He was not very rich. He was working as an accountant or clerk in a bank. He was of a Polish-Irish heritage and very Catholic. His name was Sean and the last name was something ending in 'ski'. Your mother claimed she never went to bed with him, although I doubt it."

"Do I look like him?" Tristan asked.

The Old Man closed his eyes, lost in his

memories. "In a very particular way. You have the same tall, imposing figure he had. Other than that, he had reddish-blond hair and blue eyes."

"Did he disappear one day like the others?"

The Old Man laughed. "No, no, he didn't. I asked Katherine to marry me and we left Cheyenne. I've never seen or heard of him after that." He closed his eyes again and leaned his head back against the chair. "Of course, you understand that your biological father could be anyone of these three or maybe an unknown one-night stand. Only your mother knows the truth. She might tell you for a price. If you want to find out I can give you any sum you need. Either one of your brothers will do the same. You have only to ask if you need help of any kind." His eyelids fluttered and his hand rested limp on the arm of the chair. The Old Man was asleep, taking his memories with him to a world of dreams.

Later that day, Tristan was driving Eleanor and Zach to Laramie. Zach was chattering about their animals, his friends, his science projects, and the sports he was engaged in this summer. He was such a nice, well-adjusted boy, Eleanor thought. It would be such a shame to be disturbed by the untimely interference of an uncaring mother. He should have been allowed to keep his dreams of an ideal mother who loved him. Like this, he would be greatly disappointed.

"You know," Tristan interrupted her thoughts, "I still don't understand why you, a district attorney, with a brilliant career in New York City, chose to spend the summer, or part of it, chauffeuring a kid to summer activities in backcountry Wyoming."

For a long time Eleanor didn't answer, lost in thoughts, trying to understand this better herself. Hesitantly, she started to speak, "For the moment, my life is on hold. My career reached, not a dead end, no, more like a huge bump in the road...."

"And you don't know if you want climb over it," he filled in.

"Yes, exactly. I know I can do it. With the

risk of antagonizing some important people, my point is valid. The problem is I'm not sure I want to. I'm not sure it's worth it. My career goals are worthy, but following this path perhaps is not what I want to do. Do I make sense?"

Tristan, his eyes inscrutable behind the sunglasses, nodded. "Of course. We all reach a moment in life when we question what we are about to do. But why do you think you are going to find the answer here, in Laramie, Wyoming?"

"All I know is that I need the distance to put things in perspective. In New York City there is too much pressure and only one acceptable way to make a decision. All my life, ever since I was a little girl, I was in a rush. Ballet lessons, piano, advanced placement classes in high school, become homecoming queen, get into the best college, then law school, internship with a prestigious firm, get the best catch of the season as boyfriend, organize the most jaw-dropping wedding, get on track to be elected judge. I have a lot of stamina for this marathon way of living, but coming here, seeing in Annie's eyes what true happiness means, I wondered if a marathon life is what I want and will it ever end? In the end, will I find, if not happiness, then at least peace of mind?"

"Most people here are simple cowboys. We don't question our daily life. If the animals are healthy, our livelihood secure, we consider ourselves happy."

"Yes, well, I decided it is high time to stop running and take a break. To take a step back and relax for a while, smell the roses, as they say." Eleanor laughed, looked at Zach in the back seat and continued in a low voice, "Zach is asleep. I think our talk bored him to sleep."

They fell into a companionable silence. Tristan, looking straight ahead at the asphalt lane of the road was thinking that perhaps his life was not as simple as he claimed. With Zach's mother in town and his wish to find the truth about his parentage, life was bound to become complicated. Not to mention what was he to do with this beautiful woman who had decided to take a break right in his house. He was grateful for her help watching over Zach, but it seemed she was not aware of the explosive physical attraction between them. Tristan was only human. What red-blooded male could resist this siren planted in his house? In the end, he would be the one burnt and left behind, when she decided to go back to the high life in New York City.

It so happened that Eleanor was very much aware of the potent physical reaction she had to Tristan. How could she not? He was tall and well-built, dark and sexy, with soulful eyes that seemed to see through the calm she presented to the world, the tormented, confused person that she was. Every touch of his hand brought an electric zing through her and his kisses ignited her senses like no other. Why him and not James, who was extremely good-looking and sexy too? Tristan was less polished than James, educated, but at core he was a wild, hard-riding cowboy. Why him?

Apart from this sex-appeal, Eleanor knew next to nothing about him, except that he was a great father and Zach was the light of his life and that he loved all animals and was genuinely caring. Did she even want to know more? Living together might be a recipe for disaster. Instead of helping her make a decision about her life and career, it could make things more muddled and complicated.

"Are we there yet?" Zach asked in a spoiled little boy voice, startling them both from their thoughts. They all laughed.

At home, Eleanor was surprised by how large the house was and how spacious every room seemed. In the city, space was at a premium. A two bedroom apartment was considered a luxury in Manhattan, even if the rooms were small and you needed to be creative to have some storage space. Here, everything was on a grand scale. The country style kitchen was huge and very warm and welcoming. Except for the blinking light on the landline phone. A message.

Tristan had a premonition that it was nothing

good. People bring good news in person and leave a message when they have a bad announcement. Besides, friends and family contacted him on his cell phone.

He pressed the button and a throaty, unpleasant voice said, "Tristan darling, it's time you and I got together again. After all I am Zach's mother…" Some noises could be heard in the background and then it got disconnected.

This woman was serious in her intentions, whatever her reasons were. It was time Tristan started to protect Zach and what was his. It was time to fight back. First, he needed to be informed, to find out what was going on. Then he would know what to do.

Eleanor was rocking in the chair on the porch, wrapped in a woolen blanket. Nights were chilly here at 7200ft elevation even in July. She felt Tristan's hand on her shoulder and warmth radiated through her entire body.

"Is Zach asleep?" she asked him.

"Yes, he was tired with all the commotion about his mother." Tristan sat on the other rocking chair.

"I can't believe this sky is real?" Eleanor said. "This is a lesson in astronomy, so many stars are..."

Tristan smiled. "That's because the air is pure and visibility is better." He continued rocking, watching her. "Tell me Eleanor, why are you here? I understand that you don't want to return to New York right away and you have personal decisions to make. Also, I am profoundly grateful to you for supervising Zach's summer schedule and watching over him. But... after our kiss, the night of the rustlers, you did your best to avoid me and then you returned to New York City with your mother."

"I had to tie up some loose ends and repair the damage my canceled wedding caused my mother, like pay for expenses, send regrets and explanations to all the people invited, that kind of thing."

"Was your fiancé very upset?"

Eleanor burst into laughter. "Not at all. Dear James was embroiled in an affair with a woman from his parents' social circle and only too happy to be free again. The return of the engagement ring cheered him up even more because he was short of funds at the moment. Margot, his current girlfriend, has expensive tastes."

"How can a man not be unhappy to lose you? You are one of the most beautiful women I know. I'm not trying to offer cheap flattering words. You know you are beautiful and smart. Was he blind?"

"Thank you. James is a very good-looking man himself and he comes from a wealthy family. In the beginning, he was proud he found a woman to match him in looks. But he failed to see the woman inside this pretty shell. He was not interested to know the real me. He broke the engagement when I would not compromise in a professional decision when he asked me. I'm not sorry. He's not sorry. Only Mama is distraught about what people will say."

"Are you worried about what people will

say?" Tristan asked, genuinely curious if this mattered to her.

Eleanor shrugged. "People will gossip for a while, then go on to the next juicy subject. No, I don't care."

They looked at the starry sky in companionable silence for a while, both of them lost in their thoughts.

"You know," Tristan said in the end, "I am tough and I can take rejection. I did so many times, but be careful with Zach. Don't give him hope that you'll stay. We both know sooner or later you'll have enough of rusticating here and you will return to the exciting life in New York City."

CHAPTER 5

Next day, Tristan went to see a crusty old man, who worked as a private investigator and part time as a security person at school events, sports games, and rodeo competitions. Tristan had met him when TJ Lomax came with his charming golden retriever, uninspiring called Goldie, to the vet clinic. She had been hit by a motorcycle and the first vet he brought her to, told TJ that she would have to be put down. Tristan made no promises, but operated several hours on her and then watched her overnight for possible signs of infection. The dog survived the ordeal and TJ left a happy man.

In his lunch break, Tristan drove to TJ's office, a short distance away from his practice. Goldie came to him at once with a woof and her tail wagging, happy to see an old friend.

"How is my girl, Goldie? Happy to see me?" Tristan petted the lovely dog.

"All females are happy to see you, Tristan,"

muttered TJ from behind the mountain of papers covering his desk. "Maybe you should get married to temper down their ardor."

"Not anytime soon, but you'll be the first to know if I decide to take this step. Of course you'll be invited to the wedding. And you too, Goldie." Tristan scratched behind the dog's ear as Goldie looked at him with adoration.

"Now, what would I do at a wedding, I ask you?" TJ continued to grumble. Behind his bushy beard was hiding a man younger than he appeared. He claimed the beard was his natural disguise. "Did you come with business or only to play with my dog?"

"With business. Quite a lot of it," Tristan confirmed sighing. "I need help TJ. Zach's birth mother came to town, claiming she wants to get to know him. Nine years ago, when Zach was born, she signed papers giving me full custody and ran away as fast as she could. I don't think she's changed. Zach also said she didn't seem to have much interest in him but she tried to make him leave with her. I smell a rat and I want to know what is going on. Her name is Norah Sanders and here are the papers she signed when she left the hospital and Zach's birth certificate."

TJ frowned and examined all the papers carefully. He had a special interest in children cases, abducted, abused, or lost. Tristan didn't know why, but TJ was a special protector of kids' interests. Maybe that was why he was working to ensure security at school events. Not just to supplement his income.

"Tell me what else you need. I want to know why she is interested in Zach after nine years without even a phone call."

"I'll let you know what I find out. Could be tonight or a couple of days. It helps that she's from Denver. I have some contacts there. Easier than some cases where people want me to find lost relatives after thirty years, knowing only the name and little else."

Tristan looked at TJ, smiling sheepishly. "As to that, I have a second request. It's not as important as Zach's mother though. You can take your time at leisure to solve the second case."

"My time costs money," TJ grumbled again. "Be sure you want to do it."

"I'm sure. I'll get the money," Tristan answered. "It is high time I solve all my problems of the past in order to build my future…. As you know I was adopted by Maitland. I want to know who my biological father is."

"You don't want much, hmm? It's been what? Thirty years? Why don't you ask your mother? It'd be faster, not to mention cheaper."

"I thought about this a lot. In the past, I thought she never answered my questions because she wanted to convince Maitland and everyone else that I was his. Now I know she did it in order to control me in a warped sort of way. It will not be cheaper, she'll ask for a lot of money and in the end I'm still not going to be sure she told me the truth."

TJ scratched his beard. "Oh man, you do have problems. Do you at least have some ideas? Or do I have to find out with whom your mother was inordinately friendly thirty years ago?"

"I have three names. What I want from you is to find out if they are alive and where they live. I'll take care of the rest myself. I'll find out if one of them is my father. Thank the Lord there is DNA testing."

"What if none of them are?"

Tristan looked at TJ askance. "I'll consider my options then." He produced another folder and pushed it toward TJ. "This is what I know. You take it from here. Pointless to say that I want this matter to stay between the two of us."

"It's the first rule of private investigation. Discretion."

Tristan left TJ's office feeling encouraged. Another skipped lunch, but all for a good cause. He had to return to his practice. His assistant had come back from Montana and he could take over some cases. They were very busy and he was needed. A niggling uneasiness was assaulting his mind. He looked at his watch. Just the time for Zach to finish his basketball practice. He climbed into his truck and drove to the gym.

Eleanor had enjoyed Zach's sports training. She brought a book, one of Annie's Scottish romances to pass the time. But the other parents and relatives included her in the conversation and cheering for the teams in the mock game at the end. It had been so much fun, she had no idea how the time went by. Now Zach was talking a mile a minute about what happened in the game and she followed him smiling and wondering where to go for lunch. They could indulge in a pizza after so much running and jumping on the court. They were in the parking lot near her car when an older sedan stopped near them.

"Zach!" The woman who called him was around thirty years old, and she might have been pretty with less makeup and red lipstick. "I was so eager to meet you again," she gushed, her eyes shifting to the man behind the wheel, as if looking for approval there.

Zach looked at Eleanor, panicked. She grabbed his hand and squeezed slightly to give him courage. She stepped forward placing herself between Zach and this intruder. "Zach is not allowed to speak with strangers," she said in a frosty tone.

The other woman measured Eleanor surprised. Difficult to dismiss her, as she had both beauty and poise. "And who are you?"

"I'm the Nanny."

The woman laughed. "You must be new then. I'm Zach's mother and I came to take him for a drive."

"I don't think so. Only Zach's father decides when and with whom he goes for a ride."

The other woman came closer. "You don't understand. I'm his mother."

Eleanor narrowed her eyes. "You

remembered this now after nine years of amnesia?"

"I have more right to decide where Zach goes than you do." The woman shouted at Eleanor.

"Not so. The boy's father has sole custody and as a nanny I am delegated by him to decide. No one else. This is the law."

"And how would you know the law?"

"I'm a district attorney."

"Ha, ha, this is a good joke." The man who had been at the wheel had approached them and was looking at Eleanor with interest. "You seem to be a smart girl. Perhaps we can reach an understanding," he said, his eyes zeroing in on Eleanor's chest.

"Not with her, no. No understanding," cried the woman.

"Oddly enough I agree with this. No understanding," Eleanor said, slapping away his hand that was touching her shoulder. It was time to change the tune. She pushed Zach behind her, she pointed two fingers straight and in a swift move she struck his flabby stomach and twisted. He fell on his knees, gasping like a fish on dry land, trying to catch his breath.

"Tony darling, what did she do to you?" cried the woman.

Eleanor grabbed her arm. "Take Tony darling and run. If you're smart you'll never come back."

The woman shook her head. "You don't understand. I have no choice."

Eleanor shrugged. "We all have choices."

Meanwhile Tony still gasping for air, rose and leaning heavily on the woman's arm got into the car. The woman got behind the wheel and they drove away.

Tristan's truck came in the parking lot, just in time to see the other car speeding away, Zach jumping and cheering, and Eleanor smiling like the cat that had caught the mouse.

In the evening, they were just finishing dinner when Tristan received a text message on his cell phone from TJ, 'I got news'. Good. He had to solve

this problem soon before someone got hurt by
Norah's desperate attempts to kidnap Zach.

The house was quiet and Tristan assumed the
others were asleep. Coming out of the bathroom
wearing only his shorts, he looked for his comfy old
robe. Not in the bathroom, not in the closet. Dang!
Zach had probably taken it. Tristan tiptoed out of his
bedroom, intent on retrieving his robe from Zach's
room. Only to come face to face with Eleanor,
dressed in his old robe, going back to her room.

"Nice outfit," he muttered.

"Yours too." She smirked pointing at his
shorts, where his manhood stirred under her gaze.
She was so beautiful with her long, blond hair
flowing freely down her back, her porcelain face
devoid of makeup, and her clear blue eyes sparkling
with mischief in the light of the hallway. His
manhood agreed and stirred some more.

"E-lea-nor," he singsonged her name. "What
are we going to do about this crazy attraction

between us?" he asked raising his hand and cupping her face. There was no way he would let her go without having another sweet kiss. Their first kiss the famous night of the cattle rustling left him wanting more, much more, wanting to have all of her.

In her eyes he could read the same passionate yearning and knowing a woman wanted him with the same passion as his own was almost his undoing.

"I've never known this kind of burning desire," she confessed candidly and leaned her face into his palm, closing her eyes.

He covered her mouth with his own and gathered her closer in his arms. Waves of intense sensation went through her body responding to his touch. Tristan pulled her inside his bedroom and closed the door shut. Still holding her, his hands roaming over her smooth skin, he let the old robe slide to the floor, unveiling the perfection of her body.

"Do you want me, Ellie?" he murmured in her ear, his lips trailing fire on her sensitive skin.

"I wanted you from the first moment I laid eyes on you, cowboy. Are you going to make me beg for you?" she asked her mind muddled by the strong sensations he created within her.

He seemed surprised by this idea, even half in joke, half flirting. "No, of course not. I'm offering myself to you. If you want me, I'm all yours."

Taking her in his arms he deposited her gently on his bed feasting his eyes on the perfection of her body. Blushing under his heated gaze, she tried to pull the sheet over her naked body.

"No, don't. You are so beautiful, Ellie. Let me show you how beautiful you are." And he proceeded to worship her with his hands and lips, kissing his way down her body and making her cry out with pleasure and desire. When he reached her core she exploded in a rainbow of colors and feelings.

"You. I want you Tristan." She raised her arms to him and he came to her, filling her with his passion and intense desire, making her feel like the most precious gift he had ever received.

Later, when sated and pleasantly exhausted, Eleanor fell into a peaceful sleep in his arms, she didn't hear Tristan whispering, "Nobody wanted me, Ellie. I hope you honestly do. Sleep well." Kissing her brow, he gathered her closer and fell asleep with her in his arms.

CHAPTER 6

"Come in and take a seat," TJ invited him politely. "I made fresh coffee if you want."

Tristan needed coffee desperately after not sleeping enough the night before, not that he regretted even one of the minutes spent with Eleanor. Knowing that TJ's coffee was as black as tar and tasted awful, he refused the offer. He took a seat, scratched Goldie behind her ear and waited patiently for TJ to speak.

"Well, I'll be honest. Finding out what motivated Zach's mother to search him out after nine years, was an easy task. In the old times perhaps it would have been difficult, going to Denver, spying. Today, piece of cake. People put online every detail of their life including the intimate ones. Go to Facebook, Twitter, Instagram, You Tube, you name it and you'll find out even what they ate for dinner. So, about Norah Sanders, she is an only child, dropped out of college, party life, married twice, now she works - when she does, from time to time - in an art gallery in Denver. She is divorced and has some alimony. Her grandfather, Robert Sanders had a real estate company. He worked hard and invested wisely. He is a healthy eighty-four year old. He had five children, one of them Norah's father. Only three of his children gave him grandchildren. Six grandchildren. Norah one of them."

"I knew that Norah's family is rich. If it's true, then it's not money she is after." Tristan reflected somewhat confused about this family tree.

"Ah, here is the crux of the matter. The grandfather is rich, but he is the only one. The family fortune is his. The rest of them lived a rich man's life, but never achieved much. Most of them just sponged off the old man. Others tried and achieved at best a regular middle class living. None of the six grandchildren, four of them in their thirties, produced any children of their own. The old man wants to see his family or dynasty, such as it is, continue. So he announced that his first great-grandchild will have a million dollars to his name to start with and his fortune will be divided only among the third generation. None of the others will receive a dime."

Tristan got up and started pacing the room. His head was spinning. "You mean Zach might be heir…"

TJ leaned back in his chair. "At present, Zach is the only heir."

"Norah wants to kidnap him to present him to the grandfather to get her hands on the money."

"Something like that, only the old man is not exactly senile. I doubt he'll hand her the million directly. I bet he has other surprises in his magician's hat."

"And all this was on social media…"

TJ nodded. "Yep, with a lot of many other details and personal comments from all involved. If you need them, then I'll give them to you, but I thought to spare you."

"I appreciate it. I need the grandfather's address." Tristan said, still pacing. Goldie watched him with anxious eyes.

"Here you have it. And sit down or you'll scare my dog."

Tristan pocketed the piece of paper. "Thank you. I'll go now."

Back at the clinic, there was chaos and his associate was none too happy to hear that he would have sole responsibility for the practice for the next few days.

Then Tristan drove to the Maitland ranch where Eleanor and Zach were practicing their riding skills. It was early afternoon when he arrived there and he was surprised to find his brother Raul at home. He was in the corral, watching Eleanor and Zach riding around. They shook hands.

"I thought you'll be out on the range working hard," Tristan said laughing.

Raul smiled under his thin moustache. He was a handsome devil. Since their father placed in his name the ranch and his entire personal fortune, he was one of the wealthiest men this side of Wyoming. The local women were considering him a catch and chasing him to no end. Too bad his heart was given to the one woman he might not have. Their neighbor's daughter, Marybeth Parker.

"I left Lucky in charge and decided to stay here for the afternoon to keep a close watch on these two," Raul said.

"Any news from Lance?" Tristan asked, his eyes glued to the figures on horses, fascinated by how Eleanor's round backside clad in tight denim jeans was moving up and down in the saddle.

"No, not even a tiny message. What did you expect? That Lance, on his honeymoon with his bride, will send us reports on what he did on his summer vacation?" They both laughed. It was amazing how easily they connected despite not speaking to each other for so many years.

Tristan followed Eleanor with his eyes.

"Careful little brother, you are drooling." Raul winked at him.

Tristan shifted his eyes to Raul. "I could say the same about you." He was not smiling now.

"What do you know?" Raul asked defiantly.

"This is a small world and rather isolated. People talk and gossip. They don't mind their own business. But this is the least of your worries, Raul. I'm afraid you'll get hurt."

"I can't help it. I can't change what I feel. I love Marybeth," Raul confessed in a low voice.

Tristan patted him on the shoulder. "We'll be here to catch you if you fall. It's good to be a family again. A better one."

"Yeah, it is," Raul acknowledged. "Talking about getting hurt, how about you? Eleanor is not sweet Annie. They might be sisters, but they are different. What are you going to do when she'll go back to her life in New York City?"

All Tristan could say looking at Eleanor was, "She's so beautiful."

"Oh boy, you are already gone." It was his turn to encourage Tristan by patting him on the shoulder.

Tristan turned to face Raul. "I'm in a bit of a pickle. Trouble seems be looking for me everywhere. Zach's mother wants him back."

"You're kidding. After all these years no judge will give her even partial custody."

Tristan agreed. "I know, but I hope we'll not go that far. She wants money."

"Tell me how much and I'll give it to you," Raul answered without hesitation.

Tristan looked at him for a long time, choked by emotion. "Thank you. It means a lot to me to hear you say that."

"If Lance were here, he'd tell you the same."

"I appreciate it very much... But she doesn't want money from me. There is a crazy old grandfather who dangled in front of the grandkids the promise of a million dollars to the first great-grandkid."

"So what do you intend to do? You know we could keep Zach here over the summer and no one will get to him. I guarantee that."

Tristan considered that. "I have a plan. I'm going to confront the old lion in his den. I'm going to Denver tomorrow with Zach."

"What will you do if he wants to keep Zach there?"

"He will not. I have full custody after all and the law is the law. Besides I don't think the old man knows Zach exists. And I'm taking Eleanor with me."

"Okay, if you need help in any way, just say the word." Raul continued to look over the corral. "By the way, I have a mustang, broken to saddle that has fits and throws whoever is riding him. The last victim was Lucky. And he was lucky he didn't break his bones. The second problem I have is with Lance's stallion, which has an ugly abscess on his knee. We applied a poultice but his knee is still swollen. If you could take a look at them both..."

Tristan smiled, happy to be of help whenever an animal was in need of his care. "Let's see Lance's horse first. We want him to be healthy when Lance comes back."

The stallion was not very happy to see them as he favored his left leg. Tristan approached him and kneeling down in the hay he examined the horse's knee, while talking to him to keep him calm. "The abscess needs to be lanced and drained. Raul, could you hold him while I give him a shot with anesthetic?"

After the local anesthesia mellowed the horse, Tristan assisted by Raul and another ranch hand lanced the abscess and drained the fluid. Then he explained to Raul how to change the wound dressing.

Meanwhile Eleanor and Zach, done with their riding, dismounted and came to see what was going on in the barn. A young cowboy brought out the spirited mustang, barely able to hold onto the halter. Tristan had all his attention on the horse. He started talking in a very low voice to the horse, patting his neck.

"What is he telling the horse?" Eleanor

wanted to know.

"Nothing," Raul answered. "Mainly encouraging words like Good boy and such, but only gibberish would suffice. The horse doesn't understand. He responds to Tristan's soothing tone."

"So anyone could talk like that?"

Raul laughed. "No, not at all. It's a very special talent to connect with a horse. Haven't you heard of horse whisperers?"

The agitated horse was bobbing his head up and down and neighed, while Tristan continued to talk in a low voice, touching his neck. And just like that the mustang quieted down, and looked at Tristan who gently touched his nose. Then in one swift movement he climbed on the horse's back and rode away.

The young cowboy slapped his hat to his thigh. "I'll be darned, Boss, how did he do it? When Lucky tried to do the same, the ornery horse threw Lucky to the ground."

Still looking after Tristan, Raul shrugged.

"He has a way with all animals. He always did. I remember when he was twelve he made a pet out of a scary bull. Nobody had dared to approach that bull's pen. Tristan was talking to him and feeding him. He has a special talent."

"The animals know my Dad loves them and will never hurt them," Zach piped in.

Eleanor was looking after the rider so attuned to the movements of his horse, so confident in the saddle. She sighed. It would be so easy to fall in love with him. Their night of love had been everything she dreamt and more. He had been both gentle and masterful, making sure she knew she mattered in that moment and that she was both desired and adored. What more could a woman wish for in a lover?

Tristan came back, dismounted and handed the reins to the young cowboy. "He'll be good now. No problem." The horse butted him in the back with his head playfully. Laughing Tristan gave him a small apple.

"Just like that?" Raul asked.

"Yes, well, he had some problems adjusting, but I think he'll be good now, unless someone irritates him in some way. He is a spirited horse," he said patting the neck of the horse with affection. The horse continued to munch the apple like a placid animal, as if he had never had any fits or thrown any riders before.

CHAPTER 7

Robert Sanders lived in Belcaro, one of the older neighborhoods in central Denver, with stately homes on large lots and mature trees.

"This is a splendid house," Eleanor exclaimed admiring the old, large Tudor-style house.

"Sanders invested in real estate. It makes sense that his own house is a prime piece in location, size, and style," Tristan explained, wondering for a moment if perhaps calling in advance would have been better than surprising the old man.

Zach clutched Eleanor's hand. "It's pretty, but I don't want to live here. I don't have to, do I, Dad?" His voice trembled a bit with worry.

Tristan hunkered down in front of his son. "I don't know what will happen, but I raised you since you were born and I swear to you no one will take you away from me."

"According to the law, your father has full custody and he is the only one allowed to raise you,"

Eleanor added.

Reassured, Zach nodded. Tristan cursed Norah silently for the fear she placed in Zach's mind and for causing him anxiety. He rang the bell at the front door. The massive oak door opened with a loud squeak and an older man with rheumy eyes looked at them.

"We came to see Mr. Robert Sanders," Tristan said and advanced inside the house.

"I'll see if he is receiving. What matter do you want to talk to him about?"

"Personal," Tristan answered curtly and followed him along a dark hallway. The man entered a large room, very much in character with the house, looking like a library from a century-old mansion. Dark wood paneling covered the walls entirely, with shelves and leather-bound books all around. A massive desk occupied the center of the room. It could have been a dark, gloomy room if not for the cheerful fire burning in the marble fireplace despite the warm July day, and the two large windows, with the heavy curtains pulled to the side to let in the bright sunlight.

In front of the window, an old man with white hair, sitting in a comfortable leather wingchair, was reading.

Tristan ushered in Eleanor and Zach in front of him. The first man coughed to attract the old man's attention. When the man in the chair raised his eyes from the book, the butler or whatever he was, announced in a mournful tone, "These people have personal business to talk with you. They didn't wait at the entrance."

The man in the chair peered at them above his glasses with eyes incredibly sharp for his age. He must have been a formidable opponent in his youth, Tristan thought. Not that he could be dismissed as feeble now.

The old man signaled the other one to leave and waited patiently for the door to close behind him. Then he looked at Tristan and raised one eyebrow inquiringly.

"Thank you for receiving us, sir," Tristan said, his hand resting reassuringly on Zach's shoulder. "I am Tristan Maitland, a veterinarian doctor in Laramie, Wyoming. This is my son Zach and this is Eleanor Jackson."

"You came a long way from Laramie to speak to me." Sanders observed his eyes fixed on Eleanor, whose beauty was standing out, impossible to ignore. "Who are you?" he asked.

"I'm the Nanny," she answered. Hearing this once before, Zach didn't react in any way, but Tristan was caught by surprise and coughed to cover his laughter.

"We came a long way because our peaceful life and Zach's summer activities have been disturbed and this is unacceptable."

The old man frowned. "I don't see what this has to do with me."

"It does, indirectly. You see, Zach was born in Denver nine years ago. Both his mother and I were twenty-one years old, college students at University of Colorado. His birth mother decided she was too young to be burdened with a kid. These were her words. I convinced her to leave him to me. She gave up her parental rights and I have full custody of Zach. When she left the hospital, she left our lives too. I never heard from her again until recently." Tristan paused to see how Zach was faring. Other than hanging onto Eleanor's hand for dear life, he seemed fine. Tristan continued his story. "Her name is Norah Sanders."

Sanders' eyes widened. "You have papers to back your story? I suppose you are not so foolish to sell me a phantasmagoric tale like this without proof."

Tristan nodded. "Of course I have." He handed the old man a manila envelope with papers. "These are copies. You can keep them. Zach's birth certificate, documentation of Norah giving up her parental rights, and the Court's decision to give me full custody of him."

Sanders perused slowly the papers while Tristan continued, "A few weeks ago, Norah came to Laramie and approached Zach. Under the pretext of wanting to get to know him, she tried twice to lure him into her car to leave with her."

Sanders placed the papers back in the envelope. "Has she ever contacted you since he was born?"

Tristan shook his head. "No, sir. Never before. I object mostly, that she tried to take advantage of Zach's natural curiosity and desire to know his mother. The damage she did to him... destroying his dream that his mother is a decent person and that if she had been part of his life she would have loved him."

"Maybe she was genuine in her wish to meet the boy. After several years people change...." Sanders inquired observing Zach.

"No sir, she didn't." Zach said. "She was not interested in me. Or to get to know me better."

Shifting his attention back to Tristan the old

man asked, "Why have you come to me? I don't have any influence over what my granddaughter does."

"Ah, but you do. You know you do. You dangled in front of all your grandchildren the promise of one million dollars. This is a powerful lure for people."

Sanders frowned. "So you know about it, do you?"

Tristan laughed with bitterness. "Of course. I bet all Denver knows. This is the age of social media. Every person is posting online all sorts of stories, thoughts, facts that affect them. In a nutshell, everyone knows your business."

"In my youth, people kept their cards close to them. That was the key to winning in business or life. I could never understand young people of today," He turned in his chair, looking at Tristan again. "So you want my money."

"No, I don't," Tristan replied with dignity. "What I want is for you to repair the damage you've done. You unleashed Norah on us, you make her back away."

"How do you propose I can that? I gave my word that my first great-grandchild will have a million dollars."

"The way I see it, there are two options," Tristan answered. "You could either tell your family that Zach is out of your game for whatever reason. Let's say because you didn't know him when he was born or something similar."

"You'd give up a million dollars?" Sanders asked raising his voice.

"In a heartbeat," Tristan confirmed, looking at Zach fondly. "For our peace of mind, for him continuing to grow as any ordinary boy, well-adjusted and happy."

"Hmm, what about the second idea of yours?"

"If you want to give the money to Zach, then place it in a trust fund. He will be the only one to get the money when he becomes an adult. Like this, no one will touch the money in the next sixteen years."

Sanders continued to grumble, looking at

Zach and trying to make up his mind. "Come here, boy," he ordered finally.

Tristan kept his hand steady on Zach shoulder. "His name is Zach."

"Come here, Zach," Sanders conceded.

Tristan released his hold and Zach advanced several steps, looking at the old man with curiosity.

"He doesn't look like a Sanders," the old man pronounced, frowning.

"He looks like me," Tristan said with pride. "He looks like a Maitland...Or maybe not."

"What do you mean?"

Tristan sighed. "I've been adopted by Elliott Maitland. So there is not much resemblance there either."

A bark of laughter erupted from the old man. "You're a mongrel."

Eleanor rose to her full height. She was not going to let this old man mock Tristan for something he could not change. "Adopted children have the same rights as biological ones in the eyes of the law," she informed him in a frosty voice.

"How would you know about the law, little lady?" Sanders asked looking at her with condescension.

Before Eleanor could voice her indignation at being called little lady, which she was not, - for a woman she was quite tall - Zach was happy to tell him, "Ellie is a prosecutor in New York City. She knows the law."

Sanders eyebrows rose in two comical Vs. "Is that so? You said you are the Nanny."

"I am. For the summer I am Zach's Nanny."

Abandoning his verbal volley with Eleanor, Sanders turned to Zach. "Do you like your Nanny?"

For the first time this day Zach relaxed and smiled his endearing, lopsided smile, so much like Tristan's. "I do, very much. Ellie is cool. She does a lot of cool things like mucking the stalls and cleaning the kennels, without worrying that she will get dirty," he explained.

"Aha! I see." Sanders said, barely containing

his own smile. "And what cool things do you like to do?" he asked.

"I play basketball, 'cause I'm tall like my Dad. I do a science project about acid rain with my friend Jake and I like riding at my grandpa's ranch… Now it belongs to my uncle Raul. But what I like the most is to spend time with my dog Torro. We have a big yard at our new house and we play together…. and with our baby goat, Dolly." He finished talking and not sure if he said the right things he looked back at Tristan.

Tristan smiled to encourage him to talk freely when the door opened and a small black terrier ran in, with her ears flopping. Seeing all the people in the room she stopped. Tentatively, she approached Tristan, who extended his hand to be sniffed. Satisfied the dog plopped down in front of him, her little tail wagging back and forth. Tristan hunkered down and while petting the little animal, looked her over.

"Gigi, come here!" the old man ordered. "I

am surprised she likes you. She is very fussy and territorial. She doesn't tolerate strangers. All my family calls her 'the terror' or 'the little devil'."

Tristan picked the dog up who cuddled comfortably in his arms. "I'm a vet," he said simply. "Animals like me." Gently, he placed the little dog in the old man's lap. "She has an eye infection that should not be ignored. She needs to be treated. If you want I'll give you a special doggy eye ointment with kanamycin."

Sanders nodded. "Thank you. I'll think about what you said. Leave these with me," he said indicating the papers in the manila envelope, carefully placed on the nearby table. "Don't worry. I'll talk to Norah and inform her that she will not get the money in any case and not to harass you any longer. And..." He looked from Tristan to Zach. "... I hope you'll bring Zach to see me again. Laramie, Wyoming is a bit far for me to travel."

"Of course I will."

Zach took out of his pocket his cell phone.

"We could text-message if you want Grandfather. Here is my number."

"Text-message, hmm. What's wrong with the old phone calls?"

Zach seemed astounded. "It's way cooler this way. And you could look at my Facebook page. Dad, can I be friends with my Grandfather?"

"Sure, you can list him if you want him to have access to your page," Tristan answered, wondering how long would the old man bear this onslaught of modern means of communication.

Sanders pulled a drawer open and took out a cell phone and a tablet. Zach input his number and then explained the old man how to work with the tablet and search for his page on Facebook.

CHAPTER 8

The door opened with a resounding bang against the wall and in a cloying wave of French perfume, Norah entered the room.

"Gramps, I wanted to tell you…" Seeing the people in the room she stopped whatever she had intended to say. Her eyes widened and she waved her hand at Tristan. "You…you… What are you doing here?"

The little terrier in the old man's lap woke up and started barking furiously. She jumped down and attacked one of Norah's designer shoes. Distracted, Norah shook her foot trying to dislodge the dog. "Let go you devil. These shoes are Italian. Let go."

Tristan masked his laughter under his palm, and then started talking gently to the dog who eased her grip on the shoe. The dog barked once more, then licked Tristan on the chin before he deposited her back in the old man's lap.

Norah grimaced looking at the scuff marks on

95

her leather shoe, then pasted a bright, wide smile on her face. "Zach, I'm so glad to see you. Come to your Mama."

Zach hid behind Tristan, wailing. "Dad, you said I don't have to see her again."

Tristan blocked Norah's attempt to get to Zach. "Stop the drama, Norah. You have not cared to know him in nine years. Don't play the loving mother now."

Norah pouted. "I was very young when I gave birth to him and I was foolish."

"You were young but not a teenager. At twenty-one you knew well what you wanted and raising a child was not in your plans."

"Yes, well I'm sure any judge will understand a mother's desire to be more involved in her son's life. I plan to file for custody of Zach. Isn't that so, Gramps? Wouldn't be wonderful to have Zach live here with us?"

"Hmm…" the old man mumbled looking at Zach.

"Why don't you admit you only want to get your hands on your grandfather's money?" Tristan asked, upset that the old man was not talking.

"That too," agreed Norah, picking invisible lint from her sleeve. "The mother of the heir needs money to raise him in style. Judge Madsen, who is my godfather, will agree with me, I'm sure."

"If he is your godfather, then he will need to excuse himself from the case because of conflict of interest," Eleanor supplied this information in a calm tone. Only Tristan knew that she was boiling inside too. A small muscle under her eye was twitching involuntary. She was upset too.

Norah zeroed in. "And you, the so called Nanny, live there with Tristan freely, exposing my son to Lord knows what depravity. The judge, any judge will have a lot to say about this."

"Cut that out Norah. You are way off the mark. Where were you, a concerned mother as you claim, for the past nine years?" Tristan addressed her in a cutting tone.

"And how will dear Tony fit into this picture of a concerned mother? Besides this is not the Victorian era to assume that a woman is compromised if she lives with a man. What you're saying is not only preposterous, but downright laughable," Eleanor added.

"You," Norah turned to Tristan "you came to get Gramps' money?"

"No, I did not. I came to make sure that you are not going to disturb Zach's life any longer."

"I'm disturbing his life?" Nora shrieked. "What a notion… No wonder he does not want to come to me if you suggested this idea to him."

"I don't have to suggest anything. You disappeared nine years ago after signing away your parental rights. You represent nothing more than an egg donor. Case closed." Tristan said firmly, preparing to leave. It had been a wasted time to come here.

Norah opened her mouth to give him a

scathing reply, when Sanders cut her off with a sharp gesture of his hand. "That's enough Norah. They came to see me and I'll deal with this problem myself."

"Oh, very well." Norah pouted. "Only remember Gramps that I am Zach's mother and as such your first grandchild to give you an heir. Although why you needed him I don't know. You had us, all six of us grandchildren…." she muttered going out and pulling the door shut behind her.

In the silence that followed, Tristan wondered what the old man was planning now.

"Well," Sanders finally said, "you must admit Norah has a valid point."

"What?" Tristan exploded.

Sanders stopped him. "Zach is her son and he will be much better off living here with the Sanders family."

"This is outrageous. How can you think I'd agree for my son to live here with that crazy woman who didn't remember she had a son for nine years?"

"I could give him advantages, education, and a life you never could," Sanders persisted.

Zach, who had followed this exchange with heightened anxiety, looked at his father with tears in his eyes. "You promised me Dad that I don't have to live here. You promised."

Hugging his son to comfort and reassure him, Tristan addressed the old man, "You could never give him what he already has, a loving family and a free life, riding horses, playing with animals, and his own friends at home in Laramie. You could never make him happy. Besides, it's a moot point because I am his father and I decide where he can live."

"I could give you money..."

"Stop it. What kind of man do you think I am to sell my child? Only Norah would do that. What kind of grandchildren did you raise Mr. Sanders? Eh? Think about it. Do you want Zach to become like them?"

The old man leaned back in his chair, understanding he was not going to get his way. That was probably a rare occurrence in his life. "Then we'll let the judge decide which home is better for Zach." He said in a threatening voice.

Zach stepped forward. "You are a mean old man. I wanted you to be my grandfather, but not anymore. I will unfriend you on my Facebook page. In case you don't know, this is one of the most serious insults on Facebook, to be unfriended publicly."

His father called him back. He circled Zach's shoulders and hugged him. "If it's war you want, Mr. Sanders, you'll have war. Just remember that Zach is my son and I'll put up a mighty fight against anyone who tries to take him from me. You might be king here, but the Maitlands are quite a powerful family in Wyoming. My brothers will be behind me one hundred per cent in this fight. I don't know what your feelings are or if you have any, but you might want to consider that in this fight Zach will be very hurt and upset. You could have been a grandfather figure to him. But you lost this chance. No matter if you win or lose the trial, in reality you already lost him."

Eleanor, who had let Tristan talk to Sanders, now stepped forward. "Your scheme to take Zach away from Tristan might have worked when Zach was two or three years old, but now this attempt has no legal merit. First, because Tristan is a reputable veterinarian with an established practice in Laramie. Second, because at nine years old, Zach's opinion will matter and the judge is obliged to take it into consideration."

"You can't keep me here. I'll run away. See if I don't." Zach concluded as they made their way out.

In his truck, Tristan leaned his head on the wheel. "How could I have been so naïve and stupid to believe that I could reason with them?"

Eleanor placed her hand on his arm. "You did what you thought was right. You tried to stop Norah's attempts to disrupt Zach's life. Maybe she was even planning to kidnap him. You did the right thing."

"I opened a can of worms. That's what I did.

Fool that I am." Tristan looked out the window without really seeing.

"Stop beating yourself up. Don't forget that if you have to fight, as you said, you have a large family, three brothers, parents, and now in-laws. Annie and me. We are all behind you and… if nothing works, we'll sic my mother on them. Nobody can argue with her. They have no idea what a formidable opponent she is."

Tristan turned to look at her and a ghost of a smile lighted his face. "Thank you, Eleanor."

"Let's go home. What are we waiting for?" Zach said.

In the evening when they arrived home, furious barking could be heard from the barn. When Tristan opened the doors, two balls of fur Cleo and Toro, plus the baby goat, rushed out to welcome them with doggy kisses and more barking. The animals had been fed by a neighbor, but they had been lonely without human company.

"Welcome to my crazy life," Tristan said

laughing and entered the horse stalls. Zach was frolicking in the dry grass with the dogs and the goat.

The summer sky was as gorgeous as always, with millions of stars twinkling and a bright moon. Eleanor inhaled deeply the pure air and went inside the house to put together an easy meal for dinner.

CHAPTER 9

The clinic was full of animals in need of care and Tristan had just returned from a remote ranch where he had an emergency call about a newborn calf.

Now he was operating on a large German Sheppard dog who had stepped on some broken glass. Tristan was just extracting some deeply embedded bits of glass from his rear paw when the door to the examining room opened suddenly, making the dog's leg jerk despite the anesthetic shot he had been given.

"Trish, you know better than to interrupt me during an operation. Please close the door."

"It's not that flighty Trish, darling. It's your mother," Katherine Maitland said, making him almost drop the glass shard. Swearing inwardly things not meant for his mother's ears, Tristan placed carefully the glass piece on the tray and said clearly. "Please wait in my office until I finish this operation.

I can't talk to you now."

"Well, you don't have to get all in a huff. I'm your mother after all," she said in a petulant voice.

Tristan made sure there were no more glass shards in the dogs' paws, cleaned them with antiseptic, and bandaged him. After assuring the owner that the dog's wounds would heal, he went to his office to face his mother.

When Tristan entered his private office, he found his mother rummaging through his drawers. His mother didn't know the meaning of the word privacy. Everything she was interested in was fair game. She pushed the drawer shut and without embarrassment or issuing any apology for being caught, she went straight to her subject of interest.

"Tristan, I need money." She sniffed twice, dabbed at her eyes with a tissue, and went on with her performance. "You know how callously your father treated me. After being his devoted wife for twenty-six years, this is my reward."

Knowing he was in for a long drama, Tristan

pushed the papers on his desk aside and tried to lean and half-sit on the corner of his desk. In the small room, there was only one chair, behind the desk, and his mother occupied it. He'd be darned if he stood up in front of his own desk like an unruly student waiting to be punished.

"What reward is that, mother?"

"Don't pretend you don't know, Tristan. The ranch should have been yours. When that Mexican bastard was given everything, the ranch, the house, the money, I had to leave. How could I have stayed there with him lord and master?"

Tristan nodded in agreement. "For all involved, it was better that you left."

His mother's dark eyes lighted with an inner fervor. "But I have plans. I'll file for divorce and I'll sue the Mexican for every penny he has."

"You'll lose," Tristan commented in a flat tone. "Raul is Maitland's biological son and Maitland has every right to leave him his fortune."

"But I'm his wife. I lived with him all these

years…"

"He has documents proving that you siphoned a lot of money into your personal account. He can prove that you had your share of the family fortune."

"Lies, all lies," Katherine cried.

Tristan sighed. It was embarrassing for him to talk about certain facts with his mother, but it seemed that it could not be avoided. "If you add to this the fact that he can prove you were unfaithful to him for years with Cole Warner, then you'll lose for sure."

Katherine narrowed her eyes. "He told you lies so that you, my own son, would turn against me."

"Mother, I'm thirty years old. I've been on my own for a long time. I have my own opinions." He looked at his watch and hoping to shorten this pointless conversation told her, "I'm sorry, but I have patients waiting for me. If this is all, then I have to go back to the examining room." Where on earth was Trish when he needed her to hurry him up?

Katherine grabbed his hand. "Tristan, I need money. Several thousand, five let's say, ten would be better, but five will do for now."

Tristan shook his head. It was so difficult to refuse his own mother, but he had his son to think about, not to mention a hefty house mortgage payment and now a lawyer to hire. "No, I can't. You had money when you left Maitland. I can't help you." He couldn't give in because he knew that like a blackmailer, she'd come back for more. Again and again.

She drew back, stunned. "How can you refuse me?"

He considered explaining that he had his own problems and priorities, but what was the point? He didn't have to excuse himself for having his own life. Just like it never occurred to her to explain where had she spent all the money she had taken from Maitland. Knowing his mother, he was sure she still had some, only not as much as she wanted, but a decent amount to live in comfort. Besides he was not going to finance a vendetta against his brother Raul.

Katherine narrowed her eyes in a calculating

manner. Ah, Tristan thought, if pleading didn't work, bargaining was the next step. His mother was and would always be a survivor.

"I could give you in return something you want very much," she said. "The name of your real father. What do you say?"

"I say that knowing who is my biological father should not be a reward for good behavior. You should have told me a long time ago if you really cared for me. When you finish the money, what will you do, come back with another name? No, thank you."

"Oh Tristan," she wailed, "How can you be so callous, so uncaring?"

"Good-bye, mother," he said softly and went back to his examining room where a calico cat with a temper, hissing and meowing, was waiting on the table.

Eleanor had problems of her own. After Zach finished his wrestling practice, which was less fun than the basketball sessions in her opinion, she treated both boys in her care, Zach and his friend Jake, with a cheeseburger and fries at Burger King, the boys' choice. She closed her eyes and instead of counting calories and grams of fat, she enjoyed one herself. Later, at home, she was watching both boys throwing Frisbees at the two dogs who were too small to catch them. She had promised Jake's mom to let Jake stay with them until evening.

Her phone rang and without checking the caller ID she answered. "This is Eleanor," she said distracted as her dog Cleo running after the Frisbee, tumbled in the grass, paws in the air.

"Eleanor, it's so good to hear your voice again," James trilled cheerful at the other end.

"Is it? The last time we saw each other I gave you back your engagement ring and you said you did not want hear from me ever again." Eleanor reminded him.

"Yes, well, maybe we were both too hasty."

"By the way, how is Margot?"

James coughed twice before announcing in a mournful tone, "She left with a Frenchman for Paris… How about you? I thought you'd be tired by now of seeing only cows and cowboys and you'd be ready to return to the civilized world."

A picture of Tristan riding the wild mustang came to Eleanor's mind, then Tristan playing with Zach and the dog, or Tristan naked rising above her, his powerful torso sculpted like a Greek God carved in marble. She turned to the wind to cool her blushing face.

"No to all of the above. I love it here and I am taking a sabbatical for the rest of the summer."

"Don't take too long Eleanor. You will be happy to know that you were right to prosecute that punk as an adult; my father said so." He lowered his voice and Eleanor could barely hear him. "His father, the banker, is being investigated for fraud. What is the world coming to? If we can not rely on respectable people, then what?"

The question was rhetorical, but Eleanor

answered it anyhow. "The world will be fine, James, as long as people are judged by their actions and not by who they are related to. The young man, a few months shy of eighteen, had to be tried as an adult because he was not sorry for trafficking drugs in school and expected his father to get him free. I could not allow this in all good conscience."

"And you've been vindicated. You were right. You come home and the judge position is yours. I am here for you. Just don't take too long…"

"Or another Margot might come up," Eleanor filled in laughing, although it was not a laughing matter. If she had married James, then another year down the road he would be cheating on her. She had been lucky and had a narrow escape.

"Come on, Eleanor, we were great together. Admit it."

"Yes, we were, both good-looking, moving in the same social circle, getting along reasonably well, but there was also something important missing."

"Sex was great. What else could be missing?"

he asked puzzled.

Eleanor sighed. "Love. Love was missing."

"Love?" he scoffed. "Are you in one of Annie's romantic dreams?"

Not bothering to explain more Eleanor ended the conversation. "Good bye, James."

Later that evening, the house was silent. Zach was probably asleep. Eleanor was rocking in her favorite chair on the porch looking at the magnificent stellar display in the Wyoming sky. And then she felt his presence. Tristan was leaning in the doorway, his dark eyes smoldering with desire. Her body was suffused with heat and she went all soft and ready for him.

CHAPTER 10

"I heard your Mama was in town." TJ muttered from behind the ancient computer screen in the middle of the mountain of papers on his desk.

"TJ before we talk about anything else, I need a good lawyer. Do you know one you recommend?" Tristan asked his old friend, petting Goldie who was resting at his feet.

TJ raised his eyes. "The old fox Sanders was not so amiable or friendly after all?"

Agitated, Tristan stepped over Goldie and started pacing the room. "I think you disagreed with my plan to go to Denver to confront him, although you didn't tell me so, but I felt it. You were right. It was totally idiotic to go. Raul told me too. Now Norah will sue for custody and Sanders will support her. He told me he could offer much more to Zach then I could. He wants Zach to live with them." He ruffled his short dark hair with his fingers, then stopped and turned to face TJ. "I can't let this happen. It's unthinkable. What can I do?"

"First, sit down. You give me a crick in the neck. Here…" He handed Tristan a card. "This is the best lawyer you could have. Just in case. Because I don't think it will come to that."

"What? Of course it will. Sanders told me so himself that the Denver Judge will decide which is a better place for Zach to live. He implied of course that he knows this judge personally, so what chance do I have?"

TJ snorted. "He was testing you. The truth is neither he nor Norah has any chance to gain custody of Zach. Even if the judge were to ignore Norah's less than maternal character, Zach is old enough that his opinion will matter."

"That's what Eleanor said."

"Ah, a good legal head on her shoulders. Too bad she didn't take the Wyoming bar exam. Anyhow, you can contact this lawyer, although I could give you in writing that after one or two other bullying attempts, Sanders will accept your decision. No judges or trials involved."

"I hope you're right." Tristan said a little more relaxed, petting Goldie who rested her head on his knee, looking at him with soulful eyes.

"Now, let's talk about the other problem. I assume that your mama did not come to tell you who your father is."

"She offered to tell me for a price. I turned her down."

TJ wrinkled his nose considering this. "Why does she need more money? Maitland let her go with a hefty account. He also pays her a monthly alimony, which is more than any sane judge would impose on him."

"I have no idea why she does what she does and frankly I doubt she knows either, considering that all her life she was dissatisfied and unhappy. Enough about my mother. Tell me what you found out."

"This was not as easy as finding out about Norah. What I can tell you is that all three men that

possibly could be your father are alive. First, I
researched Walter Dunn, the gambler. He was born
in Cheyenne and at one time was a well known
patron of the bars. This is when your mother met
him. When he was around thirty, he realized that
Cheyenne was a small town and the regular gamblers
were wary to sit at a table with him because although
nobody accused him straight, people knew he was
cheating. So he went to Las Vegas. The city fit him
like a glove, only in short time he realized that in
order to play big games he needed big money. And
he was dirt poor. He was very handsome and
charming and he started to escort older, rich women
to the casinos. Until one night when the police caught
him pawning some jewelry that was not his. He did
two years in prison for this and when he got out he
left for California and a life of parties. That didn't
last long because after one such party, on a dare, he
took a Ferrari on a joyride in Malibu. Being
somewhat intoxicated he ended up in a ditch. He was
sentenced to five years for this escapade as a repeat

offender."

Tristan buried his face in his hands. "Maybe I shouldn't dig this out. Who cares who my father is?"

"Good news is, I don't think he is your father. But, because he lives in Cheyenne now...."

"What? No more stints behind bars?" Tristan asked.

"In fact, there was another small one, when he left a drugstore forgetting to pay for his toothpaste in Oregon, but that was the last one. After that, he inherited a small antiques store from a relative and he returned to Cheyenne, where he lives now as a respectable business owner. He is not your father, I'm sure. But it's less than an hour drive and it will be good for you to meet him and perhaps to find out more details about your birth. Go see him Tristan."

"Wait, what about the other two? Maybe it's more probable one of them is my father. I should not waste my time with this one."

"Look, you gave me this list. Go to see this one first."

Not very happy, Tristan agreed.

Eleanor was much more eager to go to Cheyenne than him. For her it was a mystery to be solved and she considered that whatever murky past Tristan's possible father might have, didn't reflect badly on Tristan at all. Zach was disappointed not to be included in this visit, but Tristan ruled out getting him involved. A grandfather that had been in prison three times for various offenses was not a person Zach needed to meet. Zach became a lot more cheerful when he realized he'd spend the day at the Maitland Circle M ranch.

At the ranch, Tristan found his brother Raul in the barn unsaddling his hard-ridden horse. He nodded curtly at Tristan and went back to his task.

"I left Zach with your mother, but I guess he'll come here soon to pester you. I hope it's okay to leave him here this afternoon."

"It's okay," Raul snapped at him.

Tristan stepped back. It had been only four months since he made peace with Lance and Raul.

Old misunderstandings had been explained and resentment set aside. A warm friendship, if not yet brotherly feelings, connected the three of them. But trust was a fragile thing and Tristan's old insecurity was back.

"Zach and I, we don't need to stay where we are not wanted," he said in a quiet tone that hid the hurt inside.

Raul turned to face him and Tristan was shocked at the deep despair he saw in his eyes. Raul shook his head. "I'm sorry, Tristan. Of course Zach is always at home here. My mother adores him as the only child to spoil. And you are my brother. Sorry, it was a bad day."

"Not rustlers again, I hope."

"No, no." Raul guided his horse into the stall and turned back to Tristan.

"Do you have problems with the old man? Or my mother?" Tristan asked. His mother could bring to tears a whole army of cowboys if she decided to make their life miserable.

Raul closed his eyes for a second. The idea that his strong, confident brother could be so affected stunned Tristan. When Raul answered his voice trembled with emotion. "It's Marybeth. We are not teenagers. I'm thirty-six years old, and we could have a good life together. She has problems and she doesn't trust me to fight for her."

For a moment Tristan hesitated to speak his mind. "Tell me to mind my own business if you want, but I've known Marybeth and her sisters since we were kids and she works for me at the clinic. She is great with the animals by the way. I don't think it's you she doesn't trust. I think she believes her fate is not to be happy…. I don't know how to explain…"

"Did she talk to you about her problems?"

"No, she never did and I didn't ask. But I feel that the accident that scarred her changed her. That's why she doesn't accept your love and support. Because she believes that she cannot and will never be happy. Frankly, I think she needs counseling. She needs professional help."

Raul struck the nearest post with his hand. "You think she's crazy…"

"No, of course not. I hired her, remember. What I think is that she needs a professional counselor to make her understand that the accident was only that, an accident, and that she can be happy and have a fulfilled life. To give her a boost of confidence. The Parkers should take her to counseling."

Raul snorted. "Ha. The Parkers have other pressing matters on their hands now, not to worry about Marybeth."

That made Tristan curious. "Rustlers?"

"Rustlers would be easier to deal with. No. It's Faith. Their eldest daughter decided she wants to be a singer on Broadway, in New York City. I wonder if they blame Annie for this."

"Our Annie? Lance's Annie? Why would they blame her?"

"For telling Faith stories about the glamorous life in New York City perhaps."

Tristan laughed. "This is absurd. Ever since I remember Faith, she wanted to be a star, to sing and dance. She has a superb voice and she is very beautiful, you must admit."

Raul shrugged. "Beauty is as beauty does. What I remember is that she was very conceited and snobbish, with her nose high in the air like everyone around smelled bad. She treated all the cowboys with disdain. Me in particular, the bastard son of the Mexican cook was not worth talking to."

"Come on. She was not so bad."

"Yes, she was. In a way, it was her fault for Marybeth's accident that scarred her. But I guess she treated you differently considering you where Maitland's heir apparent at the time." Raul examined him with curiosity. "Were you ever considering Faith Parker as your love interest? I mean she is beautiful, it's true."

"No, it never occurred to me to fall in love with Faith. When I was a kid, I adored your mother who sneaked cookies to me and was the only one nice to me. Later, in high school, when I started considering girls, I liked a girl in my chemistry class in Laramie, who had a very cute dog, but her boyfriend was the running-back on our football team so I never asked her out. I guess I was a bit immature at the time."

"You certainly made up for it in college."

"That's true. Having a kid at twenty-one will make anyone mature overnight."

Raul looked at him with affection. "But things are going well now."

"If you consider that Sanders is threatening to sue for custody of Zach and one prospective father is a gambler and ex-con. And that I'm falling for a woman whose life and career is in New York City. Add all these up and tell me how well are things going in my life."

"Not easy. But life is not easy. If you need help of any kind, Lance and I are here for you. Remember that."

CHAPTER 11

The antiques store was rather small, but had a central location. An old fashioned bell above the door announced their entrance. Eleanor looked around with curiosity. She had a minor in history and old things always appealed to her, not to buy them, but as interesting mementos of eras gone by.

The store, unlike others of its kind, was very clean; the shelves and furniture polished and the glass and porcelain objects sparkling. It required a tremendous amount of work to keep it clean, but somebody took the trouble to do it every day.

Tristan approached the counter where a young woman was typing at the computer. "Excuse me, I would like to talk to Mr. Walter Dunn. This is his store, isn't it?"

The woman looked him over, smiled coquettishly at him, and said in a sultry voice, "Yes, it is. You are in the right place."

Eleanor abandoned her study of a Wedgwood

cup and came closer to Tristan. "Isn't that nice, dear?" she said wrapping her hand around his arm possessively. Tristan looked at her raising one eyebrow in a mute question. Her veterinarian cowboy was completely unaware of how sexy and attractive he was.

The woman at the counter sighed. "Walter is in his office in the back. Second door on the right." Then shrugged and went back to her computer.

They knocked on the indicated door and a raspy voice bid them to enter. Warned that this man was the most likely of the three men to resemble Tristan, Eleanor was surprised to see no resemblance whatsoever. The man behind the desk was in his sixties, but looked much older, thin, stooped, and with a mop of white hair like Einstein that could use an expert's haircut. Tristan was examining him with the same curiosity.

"Sir, if we could have ten minutes of your time," he finally said.

"Are you from the Bolger's estate?"

"No, we are not." Eleanor advanced in front of the desk pulling a chair to her. She pushed Tristan to sit and looking around she found two empty crates with which she improvised a makeshift chair for herself. "We are here on a personal matter. I'm Eleanor Jackson and this is Tristan Maitland."

It was hard to guess what Tristan was thinking meeting the man who could be his biological father. His face was inscrutable, but she knew the turmoil inside.

"I was born in Cheyenne thirty years ago. I was adopted when I was four years old and I don't know who my father is. I decided I would like to know more about the circumstances of my birth. My mother's name is Katherine. McNamara was her maiden name. Maybe you remember her."

"Katherine? You are Katy's little boy?" Dunn's eyes sparkled with interest. "Of course I remember dear Katherine. She was the soul of the parties, so full of zest for life, throwing herself wholeheartedly into any adventurous enterprise we concocted. Ah, the energy of youth! Where is she? I looked for her when I returned to Cheyenne, but I couldn't find her."

"She lives in Denver now. So you remember her. I assume you had been rather close then, thirty years ago…"

"Close…" Dunn snorted. "I loved her. She was vivacious and witty, dazzling us with her 'joie de vivre'."

"So, what happened then?" Eleanor asked.

"Bah! What happened was I asked her to come with me to Las Vegas and she refused me flat. She was in love, you see. In love with a dour, boring rancher from somewhere near Laramie, who came to Cheyenne now and again. He was using her and not even making any effort to be nice. But she had high hopes to turn him around. So she remained here and wilted waiting for Maitland to make up his mind." A moment of silence followed and Dunn looked at Tristan. "You look like her. What did you say your name was?"

"Maitland. Tristan Maitland."

"Well, I'll be…She married him in the end."

Tristan nodded. "Yes. When I was four. He adopted me. But you are wrong, she was not in love with him and I'm not his son."

Dunn slapped his hand on his desk. "I am right. I remember it as if it were yesterday. You see the memories of my youth kept me alive in… later on, in more difficult situations. This is the truth. Katherine was head over heels in love with Maitland and lived for the moments when he came to Cheyenne. Two-three days every two-three months. He was mourning his dead wife instead of looking at this vibrant, beautiful woman who loved him. And you are his son. "

"I don't know if she loved him, but I was told she had a lot of men who were close friends…" Tristan looked down at his knotted fingers embarrassed. "You were one of them after all."

"Me?" Dunn squeaked. "We were friends, yes, but I never slept with her. Are you kidding, boy?"

"Would you be willing to take a DNA test then?"

Neatly turned, Tristan, - Eleanor applauded in her mind.

"I'll take all the tests you want, but I'm telling you..." Dunn started to say, when a round, short middle-aged man entered the room. He was bald and his eyes twinkled merrily behind wire-rimmed glasses.

"I finished with the coins Wally. Are you ready to go to lunch?" Seeing the office full of people, he stopped in the doorway. "Pardon, I had no idea you were busy."

"Come in, Tripp. Come meet some relatives of a dear friend from my youth. I told you about Katherine." Dunn said looking at the other man with affection. "Tristan Maitland and his... girlfriend. Pardon an old man, I forgot your name. And this," he said pointing at the shorter man "... is my partner in business and in life, Tripp." He turned to Tristan.

"About that test, anytime you need me I'll do it." He laughed. "Please leave me Katherine's address. I miss the old girl."

Later, after Eleanor dragged a stunned Tristan out the door and into the first Starbucks they found on the street, they savored a coffee before driving home to Laramie and absorbing all they found out that day.

"I can't believe TJ let me come to talk to him knowing he is gay. Because I'm sure TJ knew it." Sipping slowly his hot Mocha Tristan remarked bitterly, "What a waste of time."

Eleanor leaned back in her chair and looked out the window at the people dressed mostly in western clothes. "Not really, not a waste. You found out many new, interesting things."

"If TJ had told me, I would have eliminated Dunn from the list without driving here."

"Tristan," she admonished him. "Don't be upset. I think it's very important that your mother was in love with Maitland and the Old Man had no clue. Is it possible for a man to be so blind for so many years? And how come your mother never enlightened him?"

"I don't think my mother ever loved anyone other than herself. Not Maitland. I don't remember them holding hands or looking at each other with love or at least desire. I don't remember kind words or spontaneous gestures," he said looking at her hand stuck under his on the table, slowly rubbing against his palm.

"Maybe she had reasons to hold back. Who knows? Maitland's indifference..."

"Maitland's indifference was not a good reason to cuckold him with the foreman Cole Warner for years. That was despicable."

Eleanor looked into his eyes. "That is what you blame her for? That's why you are not close?"

"That too. But I blame her most for instigating me, a stupid kid of eight, to challenge Lance to ride the wild mustang, when she knew that

Shorty Barnett had placed a burr under the saddle. For all the guilt and nightmares I had, agonizing that Lance might lose his leg because of me. I can't forgive her that." Tristan's voice had a tremor, proving his intense feelings. "She pretended everything she did was for me, when in fact she used me for her own purposes. She waved me in front of Maitland implying I might be his son, knowing that the Old Man wanted an heir to his precious ranch. What a disappointment I was to her wanting to be a vet instead of a rancher."

"Don't paint her only in black, Tristan. People are complex beings, not simple. For instance I believed this guy, Dunn, when he said she did not sleep around. She certainly didn't sleep with him, yet Maitland believed so. Are you sure Maitland is not your father? Maybe you should test him first."

After a moment lost in thought, Tristan answered, "I'm sure. I can't explain how I know. There was never a deep connection between us like father and son. He was always fair with me. I could say he treated me better than he treated Lance or Raul. I know and he knows that he is not my biological father. I don't need DNA tests. Unless I exhaust all my other options and want to check this one out for sure."

"The strange thing and maybe the key to their weird behavior is this, if your mother loved Maitland and didn't sleep around, then why did he believe that she did?"

"Because manipulating witch that she is, she paraded all her male friends in front of him. Maitland told me so. She made no secret of having a lot of close male friends. Probably from a misguided intention to make them all jealous. Who knows?"

Eleanor sipped the last of her coffee. "Let's hope we'll find out in our next trip to visit the next potential father. Let's go home, cowboy."

Tristan grabbed her hand to get her attention. "Ellie, would you play such games with a man you might be interested in?"

She looked at their entwined hands. "No, of

course not. I am a very straightforward woman. If I love a man, then I don't play games. I promise you that much. But then I am a very independent woman. I have my life, my career. I am not forced by circumstances to play games. For that same reason, I don't cheat."

"Tell me why not."

"Because I don't have to. When I love a man I stick with him because I want to, not because a piece of paper says I'm married to him."

"You are a very special woman, Eleanor Jackson. I'm a lucky man to have found you. I thank my lucky star for the day when Zach told me he found a crying girl outside my clinic and she might be hungry."

Eleanor laughed. "Noo, he said that?"

"Yes, and I thought you were a poor hungry homeless and gave him twenty dollars to buy food for you."

"This is hilarious. I had no idea why he wanted to give me money."

"He was upset when you refused so I suggested maybe you'll agree to work cleaning the kennels and stalls instead for the money."

"I had fun, although it was dirty work. That's why you offered me money when I finished."

He confirmed and touched the tip of her nose with his finger. "Imagine my surprise when I saw Zach's homeless girl driving away in the most stylish Mercedes that I could not afford."

Still laughing she rose to leave. "Let's go home."

CHAPTER 12

It was a beautiful summer day and the veterinarian clinic was busy and noisy as usual. After a day of absence, Tristan found himself swamped with work as his associate went to see a sick horse at one of the nearby ranches. His associate was bound to come back anytime now and share the clinic work.

He had just finished patching up a calf that got caught in barbwire and the owner was trying to make the calf get inside the trailer to take him home. The calf mooed piteously and hid his nose in Tristan's white coat.

"He sure took a liking to you, Doc," the rancher said wiping perspiration from his brow. "You talk to animals as if they can understand you."

Tristan laughed. "It comes from having two older brothers who didn't want to talk to me when I was a kid. So I talked to animals and discovered that they liked my company."

The trailer was too narrow. If Tristan went in

first with the calf following him, then he would have no way to come out. The rancher pushed the calf from behind and Tristan encouraged him forward until finally the calf was inside the trailer and the rancher pushed the door shut. "This one is an ornery one, always getting into trouble. Last week he slipped into a ravine and it took four of my cowboys with ropes to get him out."

"He's not ornery; only a curious fellow. He likes to explore. Like humans, animals are not all alike. They are different and need understanding and care," Tristan explained checking through the small openings in the trailer to see if the calf was okay.

The rancher scratched his head. "If you say so, Doc." They shook hands and the truck with the trailer was on its way.

Tristan looked after the trailer and breathed deeply. He was so fortunate to do what he loved. He turned back to go inside where other animals waited in need of his care. He went inside the annex with stalls for larger animals to check on a horse, when he heard angry voices outside. He walked around the building and there he saw a rather short, heavy built man trapping his vet assistant and neighbor, Marybeth Parker against the wall. She was wailing in her hoarse voice, "No, no, please don't do this Jody."

In the same angry voice, the man called Jody yelled at her, "I will do it. I'll go talk to him. See if I don't. Unless you bring me the money, I'll do it. I had some losses lately." He shook her like a rag doll. "Do you understand? I need money. Or I'll talk to him." He raised his hand to strike her when Tristan reached them. Grabbing his wrist and spinning him around and away from Marybeth, Tristan twisted his arm behind his back.

"I don't like bullies and I abhor men who mistreat women. Marybeth is my employee. If I ever catch you around here or near her, I'll break your arm," Tristan said in a menacing tone.

"Let go! Who do you think you are?" the bully complained, trying to wrest his arm free.

"I'm the owner of this clinic, Marybeth's employer, and the one who is going to call the police right now for assaulting my personnel."

"No, no," Marybeth protested. "Please don't call the police, Tristan. Let him go. It's better this way."

"You heard her. Let me go," The bully demanded.

Tristan looked at Marybeth, who had tears in her eyes. He knew that if she didn't want the police involved, then he'd have to let him loose. "Fine. But if I catch you threatening Marybeth again, I'll break your bones without waiting for the police. Just so you know." Reluctantly he loosened his hold and the man snatched his arm away.

"Next time you'll not catch me unaware," he said with bravado, yet keeping a safe distance from Tristan.

"I'll catch you anyhow. It is a promise." Tristan was not bragging. He had been champion wrestler both in high school and in college.

"You can't escape, Marybeth. Remember that." The bully said as a parting shot and took off at a rapid pace for the parking lot, climbing into a rusty truck. On its last prayers, the engine started after three tries and with a cloud of exhaust fumes and loud engine noise, the truck left for the road.

Tristan looked back at Marybeth. Her eyes were brimmed with tears and she looked at him with… fear? Lord protect him from difficult women. "Marybeth, I don't know what is going on with you…"

"I'm sorry," she cried. "I can't tell you."

"…and I don't want to know. Don't be afraid. I'm your friend and I've known you since we were kids. When you need to talk to someone, just know that I'm here and I want to help you."

She nodded and relieved that he would not question her, turned to go.

"Please, I'm not done talking yet," Tristan said gently, but firmly. "You are a very good and hard-working employee, great with animals. I want to assure you that you will always have a job here if you need it. I don't need to know the details of your private life. But behavior like what I witnessed today will not be tolerated in my clinic. Whatever your reservations are, next time I'll call the police. Because this kind of bullish behavior, not to mention that he was blackmailing you, is dangerous. If overlooked, it can escalate to criminal behavior. It's a mistake to let him go."

"I'm sorry," she repeated in a barely audible voice.

"There is nothing you have to be sorry for. Except for letting him go. That was a mistake that will encourage him to come back." Tristan touched her arm to get her attention. Instinctively, she flinched away.

"Look, I'm not going to interfere, but you have to get your life in order, Marybeth. Whatever happened in the past, your accident and your scar, men who were less than kind to you, all these are in the past. You are entitled to live a full, happy life. Let go of the past and the unhappiness. You have friends and you have Raul."

She shook her head. "You don't know what I've done."

Tristan sighed exasperated. "No, I don't. Maybe I have no right to say this, but Raul is my brother and I don't want to see him hurt. He is hurting, Marybeth. Mainly because you don't trust him and don't let him help you. He would move mountains for you if only you allowed him to do it. Instead you allow this Jody person to bully and blackmail you and then cover for him. It is true that I don't know the particulars, but Raul is a very strong and loyal man. He stuck with Lance all these years against all odds and helped him put his life together. He can help you. Even if you don't trust your sisters, Raul and Lance and I are a force to be reckoned with. We can make the evil go away. For my brother who deserves to be happy, think about it, please."

She nodded and ran inside the annex building. What more could Tristan say or do? She needed counseling and Raul had his hands full. Tristan was afraid that this entire story with Marybeth would bring Raul a lot of grief.

Women were complicated creatures and moody and Marybeth more than others. He was happy that his beautiful prosecutor was even-tempered, no fits or nerves. It will not be easy courting her or convincing her to give up her glamorous life in New York City. And maybe she never will. Maybe for her this was only a summer interlude. But darn it, she was worth the fight.

"Tristan, we have to operate on Mrs. Moody's cat. What are you doing? Communing with nature? Come inside." His associate looked haggard, his white coat splattered with some substances better left unnamed.

Later that night, the house was quiet, Zach asleep with his little dog Torro snoring at his feet and only a cricket was accompanying the peace of the summer night. Wrapped in a blanket against the coolness of the night, Eleanor was rocking slowly in her favorite chair on the porch, savoring the serenity of the moment. The clear sky was putting on a veritable show of stars and galaxies and a splendid moon lighted a path over Laramie's high plateau.

"I knew I would find you here," Tristan said, taking a seat on the other rocking chair.

"I'm listening to the silence. Do you know how rare such a peaceful moment would be in New York City? I feel like I'm dreaming and I don't want to wake up."

In the darkness of the night, Tristan smiled. "That's because you haven't seen a winter in Wyoming."

Eleanor closed her eyes trying to conjure up a picture of the land covered in snow. Hm, beautiful. A Christmas tree, full of colorful decorations and lights. A sleigh ride in the snow, with people singing merry carols. "Tell me how is winter."

"Very cold. Blizzards can be dangerous. People can die outside if they get lost," Tristan said,

thinking of Lance's mother, the first wife of Elliott
Maitland. He looked at Eleanor; only a figure in the
dark. His Ellie was a strong woman, practical and not
inclined to unhappy moods and drama. He realized
that although not a native of Wyoming, Eleanor
would never be caught outside in the snow in the
middle of a blizzard. "Winter is also a time when
ranch work is slower and people get together more
often. Families have fun and make plans."

"How wonderful! Annie likes this
tremendously, to organize get-togethers, to cook, to
decorate. She'll be happy here."

"Ellie, have I ever told you how much I
admire you? I mean you are beautiful and when I see
you my blood starts to boil. When I touch you, I feel
the attraction like an electric jolt and I know nothing
more than the desire to take you to bed and make you
mine. You know all that. You felt it too. But what I
want to tell you now is that I admire your calm in any
situation. You are so reasonable, not prone to anxiety
and nervous breakdowns."

This entire statement left Eleanor speechless for a moment. Especially when she realized that he was dead serious. "Tristan, I have strong emotions and I am all in a rage inside when I perceive an unfairness or injustice."

"Of course, you are human. You also know how to control these impulses and use your judgment before acting."

Touching him with her hand she said, "What happened? I am flattered by your opinion of me, but I sense that something happened to bring this on. Tell me." Dragging her chair closer, she hooked her arm beneath his and leaned her head on his shoulder.

He was reluctant to speak at first, but who could he ask what to do? "Do you know Marybeth Parker, our neighbor's youngest daughter?"

"Raul's girlfriend?"

"You know that?"

"Of course I know, everybody knows. If your brother's hopeless looks in her direction were not a clear sign, then I know because I was at Lance's house the night of the rustlers when she rode to warn Raul. That was quite a kiss."

"Right. I forgot about that. Raul likes to believe it's all a secret."

Eleanor laughed. "Yeah right… Besides, why a secret? They are not teenagers. They are adults."

"I don't know the details. All I know is that Marybeth had an accident when she was twelve, which resulted in the scar on her face. After that she changed into a semi-recluse, not talking to people. She's my employee, you know? She's good with animals and hard-working. She doesn't talk much. I fear for Raul. This story doesn't have a happy-ending written on it."

"Raul is a strong man."

"Yes, but he is only a man and vulnerable where she is concerned. Anyhow, today I caught Marybeth in a squabble with a scruffy man. He was threatening to talk to someone if she doesn't give him money. She was scared and she didn't let me call the police."

"Who was he supposed to talk to? Raul?"

Tristan tried to remember exactly what he heard. "I don't know. I don't think so. After the man left, I spoke to her hoping to make her see reason. Whatever problem she has - and I don't know if Raul knows the whole truth - I told her that our family will help her. Eleanor, I'm afraid Raul is in trouble."

"First, we need to know the particulars in order to help her. I could come to the clinic and try to talk to her."

He considered this for a moment. "You know if anybody can succeed in this it might be you. Thank you."

Then he scooped her up in his arms, blanket and all, and carried her to his bedroom in spite of her shushed protests that she was too heavy.

CHAPTER 13

"Well TJ, you sent me 'tilting at windmills' as they say, like the proverbial Don Quixote." Tristan said, once he was seated in a chair, a cup of coffee in his hands. "You knew it was pointless for me to go to Cheyenne."

Taking his glasses off, TJ rubbed his eyes. "I knew Walter Dunn lived with another man, but pointless? Are you telling me that you found nothing new or interesting in Dunn's story?"

Tristan waved his hand dismissively. "I found out that my mother was madly in love with Maitland and had never been unfaithful, at least according to Dunn. I lived with them all my life and I know for a fact that love was not what they felt for each other. My mother had her own personal interests and she cheated on Maitland with Cole Warner, the foreman."

"People hide their feelings most of the time."

"Not in this case…. Now what do you have

for me about the other two? And TJ, you better tell me all you know or I'll be real mad. I'm your client and I pay for this information. I can't believe you didn't tell me Dunn was gay and could not be my father."

"Tristan, I can find a lot of things from records, social media or plainly by talking to people, but some facts only you can find. All I do is to help you put together details to get to the truth you want." TJ pushed a picture over the desk. "This is the second candidate to be your father. Edgar Hartman."

The picture, a computer print, showed a white-haired man, quite tall and on the thin side, near a golfing cart. Tristan leaned back in his chair, disappointed.

"He doesn't look like me at all. He's... just an old man." Goldie came in through the back door and with a happy 'woof' bounded toward Tristan. "Did you have a good romp outside, girl?" He patted her neck gently and scratched behind her ears.

"Of course he looks like an old man, because

that's what he is. He is seventy-seven years old. He is quite healthy and active for his age and most importantly for you, he's not senile. His memories might be intact. What did you expect? That he would be a carbon copy of yourself? He was forty-six to your mother's twenty-four, a difference of twenty-two years. Besides, you resemble your mother and her side of the family." TJ shuffled the papers on his desk and clicked some more at his ancient keyboard.

"I expected to feel a connection… a sign that we are related. I feel nothing. It's just a picture of an old man." Tristan sipped the last of his coffee and placed the cup on the desk. "All right. No resemblance, I understand. Tell me more about him."

"He was born in Durango, Colorado and worked for a mining consortium. He traveled a lot, prospected mines, invested in some. During these travels, he stopped in Cheyenne and met your mother. How intense the relationship was, I don't know, but he was very generous to her. At some point, one of his personal investments, a mine in

Montana struck copper and he resigned and moved to Montana to manage it. I suppose his visits to Cheyenne ceased around that time. He earned a fortune. After ten years, he sold the mine and added to his fortune. He never married, although he had several long term relationships. I guess, after a while and no proposals, the ladies moved on."

"Hm, where does he live now?" Tristan asked wondering how far TJ would send him this time.

"In the paradise of the rich and famous, Jackson, Wyoming. Although he is not so rich compared with his neighbors, another wise investment was a nice house on a large lot in town. Twenty years ago, when it was not so posh, one could buy a house in Jackson or anywhere near in the Jackson Hole Valley at a reasonable price. He is healthy and spends his time gardening and golfing with some friends his age. He doesn't have children, but has two nephews and a niece who watch over him… and over his fortune, I might add. You'll have to be careful how you approach him. As a long lost son with claims to his money, you'll never convince them that all you want is a DNA sample for your own curiosity." TJ handed Tristan an envelope. "You have here all the information. Good luck in Jackson while I research the third candidate."

"About that…," Tristan said while pocketing the envelope. "There is another person I want you to investigate."

"What? A fourth potential father? My advice would be to start DNA-ing Maitland first. It might save you a lot of running around."

"Forget Maitland. He's not the one."

"Why? Because he said so? I wouldn't be so sure."

"Because I feel so. No, the person I want to know more about is a short, stocky guy of about thirty, called Jody, who owns an old, rusted truck and knows Marybeth Parker. They had some history together and the guy threatened her and asked her for money or he will talk to another person. I don't know what person or what about. I want more details about this guy Jody."

TJ looked at him over the rim of his glasses. "Now you're interested in Marybeth Parker?"

"Don't be silly. She's my employee and…"

"Isn't she still stringing Raul along?"

"Jeez! All Laramie knows Raul's business?"

TJ shrugged. "Small town and all that. I'll see what I can do."

Tristan rose stepping over Goldie. "Thank you. See you when I get back."

The idea of driving all across Wyoming filled Eleanor with excitement and she clapped her hands in joy. "What a splendid summer adventure! Think how happy Zach will be."

Tristan shook his head. "Zach is not coming with us."

"But Daaad…" protested Zach. "I want to see Yellowstone Park."

"This is not a vacation, folks. I need to go to Jackson to see this guy. That is all. I can't abandon the clinic for long. My associate will kill me."

"But he was in Montana for a month," Zach reminded him.

"Yes, he was, but the practice is mine. I'm the owner. The responsibility is mine."

"This doesn't mean you are not entitled to a few days off now and again. Next weekend linked with Monday, Tuesday, and maybe Wednesday will be plenty of time to solve our problem and enjoy the surroundings," Eleanor presented a more acceptable time frame.

He could not deny that it was appealing to spend a few days to see Jackson Hole. "Very well. I'll talk to Frank and see if he could take care of the emergencies. I'll see the rest when I come back."

Zach looked from one to the other almost hopping with eagerness. "And I can go too. Isn't that so, Dad?"

"Of course he'll come with us, Tristan?" Eleanor asked in a tone that was more of a demand.

"Zach will enjoy the scenery and the drive, but we can not all invade this old man's house and life. So maybe at first you go see him alone, Tristan. We'll walk in town and wait for you."

That night on the porch, the sky was covered with some passing clouds and now and again the moon peeked through a thinner cloud lighting the plain. Then thicker, darker layers of clouds ran over it.

"It is beautiful," Eleanor whispered in wonder, from her cocoon of woolen blanket.

"Beautiful," Tristan echoed looking at her.

"We need a glider chair on the porch. So we can cuddle together."

"Come here, with your blanket and sit on my lap."

Eleanor gathered her blanket around her and gingerly lowered herself on his lap. His arms circled her. "Do you think the chair can support both of us?"

"Mm, yes, it's a pretty sturdy chair. Local

craftsmanship," he muttered, his face buried in her neck, kissing the soft, sensitive spot behind her ears. "Have you always wanted to be a prosecutor, Ellie?"

Distracted by what his lips were doing to her, she almost didn't hear his question. "Not really, no. When I was a little girl I wanted to be a ballerina."

"You would have been a superb ballerina. You move with elegance and grace. Why didn't you?" His kisses went along her jaw and up to her temple.

"I was too tall. A ballerina needs to be short or she'll be funny, taller than her partner when she rises on her toes, 'en pointe'. …ah, …and some particular steps with the partner are impossible if she is taller than him." She turned her head and opened her mouth under his. He nipped at her lower lip then soothed her, sucking on it.

"Then you decided to be a lawyer."

"Well my father had been a lawyer, so I studied law. I was a good lawyer, but when I interned at the district attorney's office, I knew I had found my calling." Opening a few buttons of his shirt, she buried her nose in the base of his neck and spread butterfly kisses down his chest.

"Why was being district attorney better than being a lawyer?" he asked, sucking in his breath when she reached a particularly sensitive spot at the base of his neck.

"I found I could be more assertive and my efforts more rewarding," she murmured returning to his mouth. Then his mouth found hers and the passion ignited like fire.

His arms tightened around her and she could feel him hard under her.

"I don't think a two seat glider would help us now," he muttered, frustrated by the restricted movements in the rocking chair. "Let's go inside."

CHAPTER 14

A small vacation with Zach and Eleanor was very appealing to Tristan and as he thought about it, the feeling of anticipation increased. His elation lasted until next day at work, where, after making all the necessary arrangement with his associate, his happiness tumbled down and fizzled out like an extinguished firecracker when a man served him papers. Norah had filed for full custody of Zach in a Denver court. He would have to deal with this after coming back from Jackson.

The drive from Laramie to Jackson was six hours long. At the end, they were all tired, although the last part from Pinedale through the mountains was truly spectacular. The city of Jackson, located in the Jackson Hole valley at the foot of the mountains was named after one of the trappers who descended from the mountains in the valley to do his trade.

It was late afternoon when Tristan went to find Edgar Hartman. His house was a log and stone house, somewhat smaller and understated compared to its neighbors, yet it had a special charm.

A middle aged woman looking ready to spit nails answered the door at the third ring. She wiped her hands in her apron and looking at him askance barked, "We don't want any solicitors." She slammed the door shut, with a resounding thud.

Friendly people! – Tristan thought. Now what? He had no phone number on the paper TJ had given him and the times were you could find a phone directory book in every drugstore where long gone. White pages were online, but you had to pay for the information giving them all your credit card data. He wandered to the side of the house admiring the colorful flower beds. The gate was open and through it he saw a man bent over an ornamental bush, trimming it with long gardening shears. Maybe he could get the information he needed from this guy. After all Tristan was not sure this was the right house where Hartman lived.

Hearing his approach, the man stopped

trimming and straightened. He was quite tall, in gardening overalls and with a straw hat covering his head. "Hello!" he said and waited for Tristan to speak.

"Hi! I'm looking for Edgar Hartman. Is this his house? The woman who answered the front door didn't give me time to ask anything."

The man laughed and his piercing blue eyes twinkled merrily. "Agnes, my housekeeper can be curt, especially if you interrupted her cooking or dough making. But she is a divine cook and so I allow her to be moody. Yes, I am Edgar Hartman. Are you from the landscaping company? I expected them to give me an estimate for rebuilding the gazebo that is rotten and for re-bordering the flower beds." He set his shears down and looked at Tristan.

"No, I'm not from the landscaping company. My name is Tristan Maitland and I'm a veterinarian in Laramie. I would like to talk to you about a personal matter."

Hartman looked at him with curiosity. "Sure.

Let's go on the patio."

The garden was exquisite, the flower beds meticulously cared for and the lawn mowed to perfection.

"A passion of mine, gardening, discovered in my older years. It keeps me healthier and more fit than any gym membership," Hartman remarked with pride.

"It looks beautiful," Tristan confirmed. The flowers thrived in the warm, end of July weather. The sun was setting, embracing the whole garden in a reddish light. Tristan looked at Hartman, waiting for a sign of … something to signal a connection, an atavistic recognition. He felt nothing. Hartman was looking at him so he started to tell his story. "I was born thirty years ago in Cheyenne. My mother's name was Katherine McNamara. There is no father's name on my birth certificate. I'm trying to find out more about the circumstances of my birth."

Hartman seemed surprised and his look became more intense, penetrating, like he too was trying to see a resemblance in Tristan. "Is your mother still alive?" was Hartman's first question.

"Yes, but she's not saying much," Tristan sighed, remembering his mother asking for money in exchange for information that might not even be true. "Do you remember her or any details that could shed light on who my father is?"

Hartman continued to look at him without really seeing, lost in his memories of a long time ago. "Did she tell you about me?"

"No, she never did. My adoptive father told me about three men who were interested in my mother and kept company with her then."

"Did you talk to any of them?"

"Only one of them. Walter Dunn. But he is not..."

Hartman's bark of laughter shook the serenity of the sun-setting garden. "Walter was more interested in me than Kate. But I remember that they were good friends, laughed and danced together. It made me feel old at my forty-six years of age. Isn't that funny? Now I feel young at seventy-seven." This seemed to transport him back in the present. He looked at Tristan with shrewdness. "So you are looking for your father."

"Yes," Tristan confirmed, wondering how to alleviate this man's suspicion that he was after his fortune. "Look, I have a good life in Laramie, a prosperous practice, a family, I have a nice kid,..."

"You have a child?" the other one interrupted him.

"Yes, nine years old. His name is Zach."

"Where is he?"

"He is walking through the city with a friend." When no more questions followed, Tristan continued. "I have two great brothers I can rely on."

"Katherine had two more kids?"

"No, no. I was adopted. We are not blood related. What I'm trying to say is - rest assured I didn't come here to ask anything from you, only to find out about my parentage."

Hartman seemed lost in thought again. "I

loved her. I had an obsessive passion for her.
Otherwise I wouldn't have wasted so much time
detouring through Cheyenne. There was no mining
interest there whatsoever. But I met her one time
when I stopped in town and I was hooked. I knew I
had no chance. She was twenty-two years younger
than me. Twenty-four to my forty-six. And this was
not all. Kate, young, beautiful and laughing Kate was
in love with a stern and sullen rancher, called
Maitland." He paused and looked back at Tristan.
"What did you say your name was?"

"Tristan Maitland. I was adopted by
Maitland."

His face was crossed by a grimace of pain.
"Ah, there is your answer. Maitland is your father."

Tristan shook his head. "He adopted me when
I was four and he married my mother. He is not my
biological father."

"He came to town and they lived together for
years at the time I was there, before you were born. I
wish I could say you are my son because I loved

Kate, but you are not."

"You were never intimate with my mother? Is that what you are saying?"

A flicker of an eyelid, a twitch at the corner of his mouth showed Tristan that Hartman was remembering more than he said. He hesitated a brief moment.

"She never gave me the time of day, yet one evening she came to the café near my hotel crying because Maitland had rejected her cruelly. I think she needed a friendly person to encourage her and show her that she was loved. I was that person. She needed me that night. It was our one and only night together. Next morning, I poured my heart out telling her how much I loved her and that we would have a great life together. I assumed naively that she felt the same way. How could she not after the night of love we shared? I was wrong. I asked her to marry me and offered her a sapphire and diamond ring. The sapphire was from one of my mines in Montana. She threw the ring back in my face and refused me. No, to all of the above. Our night of love had not been so magical for her. On the contrary, she felt that in a way she had betrayed Maitland, although she owed him no loyalty. Next day, I left and never set foot in Cheyenne again. I never saw your mother again." His eyes shimmered with suppressed tears, the memories still painful after all these years.

"So you see, my boy, I can not be your father. I'm sure Maitland is. There is your answer."

Tristan hesitated, but he needed to be sure so he asked. "If I were to sign that I want nothing from you, would you be willing to take a DNA test?"

Hartman blinked like this had never occurred to him. "Of course. I'll do it. And I don't need any signature. I'm an old man with no children of my own and a fortune that I'm not going to take with me to heaven. I have two nephews with high expectations to inherit, but if you are my son, then it's all yours by right. Only I don't think it's probable as I explained to you before."

"Very well. I thank you for indulging me in

this." Tristan extracted from his duffel bag the kit he had purchased online.

Hartman eyed it with undisguised curiosity. "Oh, you already have it."

"I bought it online, but they are available at any Wal-Mart or drugstore. It's very simple really. You scrape the inside of your mouth with it and me too and I send the probes to a licensed lab." They both did that and Tristan placed the test kit back in his duffel.

"You'll let me know as soon as they send you the results, won't you?" Hartman demanded intrigued by this possibility.

"Yes I will. Thank you again for agreeing to do this for me." Tristan rose to go.

"I have a little favor to ask myself." Hartman rose too. "Could you please bring the boy tomorrow to visit with me?"

"Zach? Yes of course I will. But why? I mean you don't believe that I could be your son, so Zach is not your grandson."

Hartman looked at the mountain peaks and the sunlight fading behind them and his eyes misted. "No he is not, but he is Katherine's grandson. I want to see him."

Later on, at the hotel, this idea was not accepted with the same enthusiasm by Zach. "Daad!" he whined in the typical way of kids who think parents' demands are a dumb idea. "Not another grandfather. You forgot what a mess it was the last time when we went to meet the one in Denver."

For a moment Tristan wondered if perhaps so much exposure to newly found relatives was indeed a mistake. Come to think of it, the old ones were no better. Zach knew Maitland and there was no strong connection between them, although it was true that Maitland was not one to openly manifest his affection for anyone.

"No, Zach. This is only a lonely old man who loved your grandmother very much a long time ago."

"Before I was born?"

"Much before your time. In fact it was before I was born, thirty some years ago."

CHAPTER 15

"I liked him," Eleanor proclaimed, looking through the window at the mountains.

"Me too," echoed Zach from the back seat, struggling not to fall asleep as it was quite early in the morning.

"Hmm," Tristan grunted, while maneuvering the car expertly through the tight curves of the mountain pass. "I'm glad you both liked him. He is a nice person and he was crazy in love with my mother, poor sod. But I doubt we'll ever see him again. He's not my father."

"What? No good vibes?" Eleanor turned to him.

"None whatsoever. I thought when I finally met my father I'll know. It will be a strong reaction of recognition. There was none. I mean, he was a nice man and that's all. Besides he told me there is not much practical reason to believe he is my father."

"He and your mother were not...." Eleanor

looked furtively over her shoulder in the back to see if Zach was sleeping. "...lovers," she finished whispering.

"Only once. He claimed my mother was in love with Maitland. The second person to affirm this. I don't know what to believe. I lived with my mother and Maitland in the same house and I know there was no love between them. There was nothing, not even hate. They rarely fought and so there was no passion or intensity in fight either. Only a serene indifference. Maitland indulged my mother in all matters related to the family or the house and in exchange he was the king of the ranch and the business. He is not an idiot. If he didn't know that my mother had an affair for years with Cole Warner the foreman right under his nose, is because he didn't care enough to be observant. There was no love there for sure."

Eleanor touched his arm to offer comfort. "That is why you started this search for your biological father?"

Tristan inclined his head. "To understand better what happened then, before my birth and also to find a part of myself that was missing. I needed to know the truth about my life in order to accept who I am and to go forward. Instead, things are more complicated and I am more confused not only about who my father is, but also about my mother. And to top it all, I have a feeling that a piece of the puzzle is missing."

"Maybe the third person on the list is the key to what you want to find out."

"Maybe, although I wonder if Maitland knew more than he said." He drove down the serpentines and lower into the valley. In the monotonous noise of the engine they were both lost in thought.

"What about you, Eleanor? I guess you never had doubts about who you are…" he said after a while, curious to know more about this beautiful smart woman who landed so unexpectedly in his life and with whom he was half in love already.

"Everybody has doubts Tristan. Not about my

parentage, but about the path I should follow in life. You see, my father who was older than my mother was a very respectable judge. It was assumed that all three of us girls will go to law school. Both Lauren and I did. Lauren because it never occurred to her to do otherwise, me because I didn't know what else I could do."

"Except being a ballerina," he reminded her with a teasing smile.

"Right, that was out of the question as I was quite tall by the time I finished high school. When Annie rebelled and announced she wanted to be a writer and not a 'serious' writer, but a romance novelist, my mother was so distressed that I knew I didn't have Annie's courage to defy Mama."

"Did you regret it?" he asked.

"Being a lawyer? No, I discovered it suited me." She grinned at him. "In fact, being a prosecutor fits me the best. I seem very in control and calm, when in fact I'm passionate and very combative. Almost like Annie, only she is more expressive than I am. I am more introverted. Men call me the ice queen for what they perceive as my lack of passion."

"I assume we're not talking now about you in court, but in life in general." When she nodded, he laughed. "They don't know you at all. I can attest at several moments when you expressed your passion quite vocally."

Eleanor glanced over her shoulder to assure herself that Zach was still sleeping and shushed Tristan. "Watch what you're saying."

Tristan smiled at her and changed the subject. "Do you know that Lance and Annie are returning today from their honeymoon?"

"The two weeks are gone already? I guess the time is flying…" she said. "I'm glad she's coming home. Both Lauren and I, we adore Annie for her ebullient, cheerful character, for her zest for life and courage to say what she thinks and to fight for what is right. When we were kids or teenagers I used to have a vague feeling of guilt. You see, Lauren and I are both tall, blond and blue-eyed girls, a genetic mixture of my father who was tall and imposing and my mother with her tiny built and doll-like features. Annie had brown hair and hazel eyes and was short. As kids, people used to look at us with admiration and discount Annie as insignificant or worse, they would ask plainly how come she was so different than the rest of us."

"It must have been hurtful for Annie."

"Later, in our teenage years, it was worse. As soon as Annie came home with a boy, he would look at us and forget about Annie. They tried to get dates with Lauren or with me. Come to think of it, Lance was the only one who gave me the attention of an unwelcome guest and had eyes only for Annie. Even Ed, Annie's former boyfriend made a pass at me a couple of times. I don't know why he thought I'd be an easy conquest."

Tristan frowned. "It shows how misleading physical features can be."

"Why do you say that?"

"I didn't know your father, but your mother

looks like a silly blond bimbo and underneath, she hides a strong will and determination and a shrewd mind. Annie looks like a curly, silly, superficial girl, and she is one of the most generous and profound beings I've met. Lance is a lucky dog to have her devotion. She brought changes to this family that I never dreamt possible."

Eleanor coughed to cover her emotion and to recover her calm. It was true. Nobody had spoken truer words about her sister. It showed her again the depth of Tristan's understanding. "What about me?" she asked him, curious how he saw her, the ice queen or the sex-crazy woman, the confident prosecutor or the uncertain person, unsure of where her career should go.

"You Ellie are a multifaceted being. I like your calm in any critical situation. I adore and crave your passion at night and that light in your eyes every time you look at me from across a crowded room. I admire your beauty because it's part of who you are. Don't hold it like a shield against misguided men.

Accept it and embrace it. You are beautiful, that's the truth. I admire your tenacity in going after the evil everywhere and not being intimidated. Of course you are also smart and bright… in a word you are perfect not only in my eyes but for the entire world out there."

Men told her often that she was beautiful, but such sincere and heartfelt words she had never received before. Eleanor wiped her eyes willing her tears to stop. She was unusually emotional these days. She was doing a good job at ignoring the truth in front of her. She was in love with the sexy veterinarian and she was pushing this truth out of her mind instead of dealing with it. Did she dare take the plunge and change her life for him? Was she as brave as her sister Annie to give up the familiar New York City for the wilds of Wyoming all in the name of love?

Lost in thought, Eleanor didn't see the change in scenery. After Pinedale, the valley widened bordered in the distance by the mountains. The high plateau again.

"Are we there yet?" a sleepy Zach asked.

"No, not yet," Eleanor smiled at him. "You can go back to sleep unless you need a pit stop."

Tristan intervened. "I think it's a good idea. We'll stop at Rock Springs and have a late breakfast." It had been too early when they left Jackson and did not eat that morning.

"A good McDonalds breakfast, Dad?" Zach asked animated by this perspective.

"Yes, a McDonalds breakfast," Tristan conceded. "No matter how often we tell these kids that a burger is unhealthy, they absolutely love to eat at McDonalds."

After the stop in Rock Springs, time passed quickly and soon they were home in Laramie.

In the afternoon, after Tristan had checked on his practice and assured himself all the animals were doing well, they drove to the Circle M ranch house were the newlyweds, Lance and Annie, returned from their Florida honeymoon, were visiting.

"Ellie!" Annie shrieked jumping down from the porch to embrace Eleanor. "I'm so glad you're still here." Annie was tanned and had a special glow about her. "Wait till you see what I brought you from Florida," she said and climbed back on the porch to arrange the pillow behind the Old Man's back, smiling at him and ignoring his scowling look. Maitland didn't like to have people fuss over him.

"How are you little brother?" Lance asked Tristan after affectionately slapping him on the back in welcome.

It was the first time in all his thirty years that Tristan was called 'little brother'. It surprised him and he discovered that he liked it very much. He looked at Raul who was perched on the corral fence grinning like a pirate and then looked around at his family ranch. This was what he was looking for, a place to belong and a family to accept him.

He almost didn't catch Lance's last words, "…I see you got the family's ice queen."

He turned to Lance. "Ellie is not an ice queen.

182

She's warm and loving and …" Lance looked at Raul smirking and they both nodded in agreement. "What?" Tristan asked. "She needed a place to relax for the summer and to decide which way her career should go. And I needed help supervising Zach in his summer activities…" Eleanor came on the porch, changed from her jeans and shirt in a flowery summer dress, probably one of Annie's Florida acquisitions. It was very out of place on a cattle ranch, but it was summer and warm and Eleanor looked so beautiful in it, the sheer fabric floating around her when she moved, that Tristan almost swallowed his tongue.

His rogue brothers' grins widened and they high-fived. Then Lance lost interest teasing his brother as his eyes slid past Eleanor to Annie who clapped her hands in delight and hopping from a step to the next climbed down from the porch and ran to him. Lance's aqua-blue eyes turned a warm turquoise and he opened his arms and gathered Annie to him.

CHAPTER 16

It was August. Although cloudy, it was rather warm and the day was pleasant. Tristan had operated on a German Sheppard guard dog with an infected abdominal wound. He was happy that the dog had responded well to antibiotics.

During his lunch break, he went to see TJ.

"Hello old man," he said entering TJ's office. "Where is Goldie?" he asked failing to see the lovely dog that always welcomed him.

"My neighbor got herself a tiny fluffy dog. I don't know what breed, but it's only a ball of fur and I couldn't make Goldie leave with me this morning. She was playing with this dog."

Tristan smiled. "Goldie is a playful social dog. She likes to visit with other animals. You don't have to feel abandoned, TJ. Better yet, you come to my office and pick another dog, to be companion to Goldie. You'll feel better with two dogs."

TJ looked at him with doubt. "I think you

want to pawn on me your stray animals, doc. How about you tell me what you have found out in Jackson."

"It was another wild goose chase. Hartman is a pretty decent guy. He had been in love with my mother, but she rebuffed him. The chances that he is my father are slim to none…. Now you better tell me what else you got for me."

TJ pushed his glasses on top of his head to see his computer screen better. Tristan wondered again if TJ really needed glasses or if it was only an affectation.

"Remember, you gave me these names. Hmm. The third one is named Sean Kowalski. Mother Irish, father Polish. He is tall, had reddish hair at one time, and now is bald like a moon. He is a very respectable citizen living in Cheyenne."

"I'm surprised. No prison record, no…"

"Stop being a smart aleck," TJ admonished him. "He is manager of the local branch of a minor bank. He married latter in life a young poor Irish girl

185

and has six children."

"Six?" Tristan croaked. There was no way this Kowalski needed a long lost son after dealing with six kids every day.

TJ scratched his head. "Some people are either very brave or very foolish. In this case, however, we are talking about a very Catholic family going to mass every Sunday. Are you sure this guy is a candidate to be your father?"

"That's what Maitland told me. I'm not sure of anything at this point. I'm confused, upset, and pissed off that I can not trust my mother to tell me the truth."

"Nobody from the past remembers this guy, perhaps because he was not frequenting the bars, taverns, and other public places."

"Then how come Maitland remembers him?"

"Maitland visited your mother at home. I think he was the only one. And if this saint Kowalski used to come to her house too, maybe that's how they met. I don't know. Do you want me to dig farther?"

Tristan waved his hand. "No, I'll go see him. Cheyenne is not far and what is one more drive?" He even envisioned a nice evening in a good restaurant with Eleanor as a personal reward after a trying day. There was no way he'll take Zach to mingle with the six kids that might be his step-uncles or cousins once removed or whatever they were.

TJ slapped in front of him a folder interrupting his musings. "This is the information. You gave me this month more work than I had in a year. Now, the second issue was about the man who talked to Marybeth Parker."

"He didn't talk. He assaulted her and blackmailed her."

"Yes, well, they have a history together. Long and complicated."

Tristan was filled with a sense of foreboding. This didn't sound promising for Raul's romance with Marybeth.

TJ continued, "His name is Jody Coates and he is currently unemployed. They met by chance, I assume when Marybeth was junior or senior in high school. Because of her scar, she had no boyfriends. She went to classes, but had no other activities and she had no friends. Boys and girls avoided her and she was alone. Her sisters were not helping either."

Tristan buried his face in his hands. "Oh Lord, poor Marybeth. I should have…"

"You were in college in Denver then, so I doubt you could have done much." TJ wrinkled his nose and hesitated. "Listen Tristan, this guy Coates is bad news. She was vulnerable when she met him and he took advantage of her, by being nice and then asking her for money." He hesitated again. "If you want me to find the whole truth I will, but it concerns Marybeth and it's very private."

"Yes, I want you to find the truth. Raul deserves to know it. To know what he's up against."

"Maybe he already knows it."

Tristan considered this, then shook his head. "No, I don't think she told him. Not the whole truth."

"Very well then. Give me a couple more days

and I'll know everything. Meanwhile watch out for her. Don't let that guy come close to her. He is dangerous. He'd been in and out of prison ever since he was sixteen."

"Thank you, TJ. I appreciate all your help." Tristan rose to go. "Well except for the recommended lawyer."

TJ leaned back in his chair. "Why is that?"

"Why? Because Norah and her grandfather will come prepared with the most famous lawyers in Denver, not to mention the judge is Norah's godfather, or so she says. And you sent me to this ... grandmother with white hair and a nice smile. And she was knitting socks at her desk. Don't you see anything wrong with this picture?"

TJ smiled wolfishly. "First, if Norah wants to reverse custody, she needs to come here, where the boy is. This is his home state. So good bye godfather judge. Second, this grandmother with nice smile is known as the Shark because she is fierce in court. What is best for the child is what she'll fight for and she'll get it. Have no fear my friend. If you'll go to an arbitration judge, she'll win the case for Zach. But I still think Sanders is toying with you."

"Norah is dead serious."

"Because she's naïve. Sanders wants a say in Zach's life. He's trying to get as much as possible, but I don't think he wants to harm Zach or to cause him distress. Don't worry."

CHAPTER 17

It was late afternoon when Tristan and
Eleanor knocked on the door of Sean Kowalski's
house in Cheyenne. The house was a modest split-
entry style so popular in the 60s and 70s. After being
embraced with the same elation as wood paneling,
the style fell in disgrace and was avoided by some
buyers for not being feng shui. It was a dilemma after
all, what to do right after entering the front door,
climb up the stairs or go down. People need a clear
direction, Tristan reflected pressing the doorbell
again. Silly thoughts to chase away the anxiety.

Eleanor didn't have the same thoughts, maybe
because in New York City anything larger than two
bedrooms and with closet space was considered
luxurious and priced in the millions. She was content
to admire the lawn mowed and edged to perfection
and some herbal landscaping well-tended. She
assumed the banker didn't have time for such
mundane chores and it was his wife doing the

landscaping.

Finally the door opened and a harried woman, wiping her hands in her apron opened the door.

Tristan gave her his most dazzling smile. "Hi, ma'am. I would like to speak to Sean Kowalski, please."

She pursed her lips and looked behind her. Then she shook her head. "I'm sorry, he's not available now. Try tomorrow at the bank."

"This is a personal matter and I'd prefer to discuss it in private. I'm sure Mr. Kowalski would too."

"No, no. He cannot be disturbed, I tell you." She seemed distressed now, almost on the verge of tears.

"Hannah, what's this noise? You know I need quiet." On top of the stairs a tall, bald man stopped and looked down at them.

"I told them, Sean that you don't receive any solicitors but they won't go," she said wringing her hands, twisting her apron.

He looked at Tristan dismissively and his eyes stopped on Eleanor with a flicker of interest. Nobody could ignore the elegant beauty. Even casually dressed in jeans and a jacket, Eleanor was stunning. Kowalski acknowledged her with a short nod of his head. However, his interest was not that natural instinct of a man who saw a beautiful woman, but more of a person who realized that she was quality and therefore it was not wise to ignore her.

"We have a personal matter to discuss with you, sir," Tristan said. "In private," he added.

Kowalski turned his eyes back to Tristan. "I don't see what personal matter you could…"

"My mother's name was Katherine McNamara," Tristan interrupted another argument. The shock and surprise showed on Kowalski's face. It froze him on the spot.

After a long, awkward pause, he inclined his head. "Come in." Then he turned to the woman. "Hannah, go to the kitchen and see that we are not disturbed," he ordered.

"Yes, Sean," she said and disappeared.

Tristan and Eleanor followed him along the hallway and into a dark, wood-panneled room. 'Well, if this is my father, then I'm glad I haven't met him before,' Tristan thought. Beside Kowalski treating his wife like a servant, there was something weird about this house. It struck Tristan that for a house where six children lived, it was unusually quiet. At home, Zach alone created more noise and laughter running after the dog, making demands, watching TV and listening to loud music. Here there was nothing. No noise, no activity.

"Is Katherine still alive?" Kowalski asked as soon as he took a seat behind his desk.

Tristan guided Eleanor to sit in the only other chair in the room and he stood behind her, his hands on her shoulders. "Yes, she is."

"Still married to Maitland?" was the next question.

Tristan hesitated, wondering how much to reveal to this unpleasant stranger. As he was going to ask him to spill the details of his youth, he supposed he owed him some truth in return. "They are separated," he admitted.

"Ah!" There was a world of satisfaction in Kowalski's voice. He nodded. "He abandoned her."

Tristan's grip on Eleanor shoulder increased and she patted his hand to calm him down. "No, she moved to Denver and Maitland remained at the ranch." Strange, he thought, this guy was the only one who knew his mother had married Maitland and so he knew also of Tristan's existence. "The reason I came here today is that although Maitland adopted me after marrying my mother, I would like to know who my biological father is. If you remember more from that time…"

"What did Katherine tell you?"

"Nothing," Tristan admitted. "She never talked about my parentage or the time before her marriage."

"Ah!" Kowalski said again as if this explained everything. And maybe it did to him. "She was crazy about me."

"Who? My mother?" Tristan croaked, taken by surprise.

"Yes, of course. Katherine loved me to distraction," he said. "It was embarrassing really. She came to the bank all the time and I had my position to consider, you understand, my career."

"Is there any possibility…" Tristan coughed. "…that you might have fathered me?"

This idea stopped Kowalski's remembering of the past. He narrowed his eyes and looked at Tristan. "Yes, of course it is possible and perhaps I shouldn't tell you this, but Katherine was very free with her favors and had many friends, Maitland among them. I guess you discounted him as father, considering that you came to me," he said rubbing his hands with glee.

"I haven't discounted anybody," Tristan replied unwilling to let Kowalski gloat. His father or not, he felt an intense dislike for this man. Bad vibes. "My mother is not talking and at thirty years of age I decided it's high time I find out who my biological father is."

"Ah!" Kowalski said lost in thought, his eyes closed, haunted by the past. "She came to me, begging me to marry her."

Under Tristan's hands Eleanor jerked, the only sign that she paid attention to the conversation. "Did she tell you that I'm your son?"

"Yes, naturally. But of course she knew I could not marry her. Even if I had not considered my career, and Katherine was not an ideal banker's wife, I was Catholic. Katherine was not."

"She might have converted for you," Eleanor said, for the first time intervening in the conversation.

"Oh, it was not possible. I needed a one hundred per cent Catholic bride." Kowalski said in the same pompous, patronizing tone that started to grate on Tristan's nerves. "So after I refused to marry her, poor Katherine had to marry Maitland and go to live on the ranch."

Tristan had heard enough. It was time to get what he came for before he got so mad that he'd antagonize Kowalski. "Sir, I want to ask you, in the interest of the truth if for nothing else, to agree to give a DNA sample."

Kowalski narrowed his eyes again at Tristan. "If you want to…"

"No, I don't want anything else but to know the truth. I'm a veterinarian in Laramie. I have my house, my family, my practice, and my own life. I don't want anything from you. I have the test here. We both scrape the inside of our cheek and then I send the samples to a lab to be compared. That is all."

"Did Katherine send you to me?"

"No, sir. She has no idea I'm doing this. I don't intend to make the results public. They are only for me, to know where I come from, so to speak.

"So, good old Maitland tested negative, no fatherhood for him, ha?" Kowalski remarked with satisfaction, proceeding to give a DNA sample as

Tristan showed him.

After that, there was no point prolonging the visit and Tristan and Eleanor thanked him politely for the sample and turned to go. It occurred to Tristan that Kowalski didn't ask to be informed about the DNA results.

Tristan opened the door to usher Eleanor out when in the hallway a small boy of about six years of age, holding a kitten clutched to his chest, stood frozen on the spot, looking at Kowalski with undisguised fear.

"Tommy, what are you doing in the hallway, bringing that disgusting animal in the house? Get a rid of it and go to your room. I'll talk to you later," Kowalski said, while the little boy disappeared in one of the rooms downstairs. "Children! No matter how you try to discipline them, they still err. One can never spare the rod, or the child will get spoiled. They need to be punished in order to be raised properly."

Eleanor looked him straight in the eyes. "I

wouldn't if I were you. Using corporeal punishment on a defenseless little boy is not discipline; it is called by the law, child abuse." This said she marched down the stairs and out the front door, followed by Tristan smiling for the first time that day and by Kowalski's sputtering protests.

Outside, they both took a deep breath before climbing in Tristan's truck.

"Ellie, do you realize that this unpleasant, horrid man has the most chances to be my father?"

Eleanor turned to face him. "He lied," she said flatly.

"You hope, but don't know for sure," he argued, barely daring to hope she was right.

"I know for sure. I'm trained for this. I can detect a very convincing liar. Kowalski lied. I don't know if only partly or if it was all a lie, but lie he did."

He raked his hair with his fingers, giving him that tousled look that she adored. "What am I going to do now?"

"You will send this DNA sample to the lab and wait for the results. The second thing that you could do is to go to talk to Maitland again. I still don't understand why you are so convinced he is not your father. He would be the most logical one. Maybe convince him to give a sample too."

For a long time he rested with his arms propped on the wheel, looking through the windshield. "Maitland is not my biological father. If I were his son, he would have married my mother right away, not after four years. He treated me with fairness always, but not with affection."

She shrugged. "That's how he treated Raul too, fair, but not particularly warm or with affection. This was his way."

"True. But I feel…"

"No more feelings or vibes, let's go for facts."

Tristan started the engine. "I think Maitland knows more than what he told me. It's time to find out."

CHAPTER 18

The small café were Tristan brought Eleanor to have dinner had a distinct country décor, with old pictures on the walls, shelves with pottery, and old tin cans and jars filled with pickles and spices. Even the tables were covered with gingham oilcloths. It was charming and Eleanor approved entirely Tristan's choice.

"Wait till you taste their food. Good, hearty comfort food," he said pushing the laminated one page menu to the side. "The day's special is always the best of whatever the cook prepared."

Expecting some meatloaf with mashed potatoes, Eleanor was surprised to hear that the day's special was Greek moussaka. "I had my heart set on fried chicken," she muttered after they had both ordered. "Eggplant is one of those vegetables that even cooks avoid. Why bother?"

Amused by her grumbling, Tristan took a sip of his beer. "Taste first, then tell me what you think, as Carmelita used to say when she experimented with a new recipe. I thought New Yorkers are accustomed to all sorts of weird foods."

"We have a large variety of ethnic restaurants and all sort of foods and so we can choose what we like," Eleanor said eyeing askance the layered square on the plate in front of her, smothered in tomato sauce and topped with melted cheese. She took a forkful and the rich, spicy taste made her close her eyes to savor it better. It was delicious. "Mmm!" she exclaimed.

"Eleanor, if you have this strong reaction of ecstasy one more time, I'll grab you, take you to the nearest hotel and have my way with you," he promised laughing. His eyes were smoldering with hidden fire, so she knew he was only partly teasing her.

"Why do you look at me like that?" she asked. "Do I have sauce on my chin?"

Tristan laughed again. "You are adorable enjoying the food like that. I love you."

The spontaneous admission startled them both. Eleanor blinked and set the fork on her plate. "Do you mean it? Seriously?"

Tristan looked outside the window. The sun had already set, although it was early evening yet, and the wind was moving some fallen, yellow leaves on the pavement. It was still the first half of August, but signs of the approaching autumn were here. And with it, Eleanor's leave of absence from her job would be over. He turned back and looked into her beautiful blue eyes. "I mean it and very seriously. I didn't plan to say it now, not like that, but it happened because this is how I feel."

"Why?"

"Why?" he repeated amazed that she would ask him. "Eleanor, you are one of the most stunningly beautiful women I have ever seen. Don't scorn me for being superficial. Your beauty is part of who you are. Accept it. The first time I touched you I felt like an electric shock. The physical attraction we feel is so strong. And I know you feel it too. Then, I love your calm demeanor and sharp intelligence. I love how you interact with Zach. This is important for me. You treat him like an adult when you talk to him, yet you play with him like a kid when you get into one of his games. And finally you love animals as much as we do and don't mind mucking the kennels or the horses' stalls. If this is not enough, then I'll simply say I feel so much love for you that I know my heart will break when you will go away. And I know you will."

Eleanor's eyes were brimming with tears. "Aren't you going to ask me to stay?"

He caught her hand over the table. "Of course. For all that it's worth I want you to stay, but I'm not naïve to think that you will. You are not ready to commit to a life in the boondocks of Wyoming as the wife of a small town veterinarian. My own life is a mess now with Norah threatening to take Zach away and with me not knowing such a straightforward thing as who my father is, where I come from, what my family's health history is. Then,

I wish I could offer you riches, but all I can offer is the promise of a comfortable life." He looked at her with sadness.

"Tristan, do you think I am so shallow? Riches indeed! Silly man, don't you know I don't need a man to offer me riches. I can work and get what I need myself. All I need is an honest, loving heart."

He shook his head. "You are not ready to commit yourself. You will leave. There is very little time left."

"Look! It's true I avoided thinking of the mess I made of my career or my planned wedding. I felt detached of all the pressure and stress of my life in New York City. Like during a vacation, I avoided making plans of any kind or decisions. I'm not sorry. I needed this mental relaxation. However, you are right. I have some serious thinking to do if I plan to change my life entirely." She grinned at him. "All will be fine you'll see."

The waitress came near their table frowning

at their almost untouched plates. "Hey, folks! Is something wrong with your food?"

Eleanor smiled at her. "No, nothing wrong. In fact, it was delicious. Could you please reheat the plates a little?"

Tristan wrinkled his nose. "I lost my appetite, sorry." He hesitated a moment. "All my life I have been mostly alone. At twenty-one I had Zach, and it's been great as just the two of us, until you came into our life. We'll miss you terribly if you'll leave. Please remember that we love you very much."

She leaned over the table and kissed him lightly on the mouth. "I love you too. Trust me."

Then he took her to the hotel and made love to her, sweet and tender, pouring all his heart into it, letting her know how precious she was and how much she meant to him. There was also a hint of desperation and fear that he would lose her. Sometimes gestures said more than words.

Next morning, they went home to Laramie. Zach was staying this time with Annie and Lance at the smaller house on Morning Star ranch. Tristan left Eleanor to visit with Annie and drove farther to Maitland's Circle M ranch to talk to the Old Man.

Maitland was in the old parlor, where he had moved his desk facing the large bow window. The room was full of light without the old, dusty velvet curtains that had covered all the windows in the house before.

"Tristan, it's good to see you. Where is that charming filly that stays with you these days?" the Old Man asked with a joviality never shown before.

"I'm glad you're in good spirits... Father. I left Eleanor with Annie." Tristan took a seat in a chair nearby and grabbed one of Carmelita's sugar cookies. "And what are you doing? You seem ...busy." Last time they talked the Old Man was bored and depressed.

Maitland straightened and said full of importance, "I'm writing."

"Writing? All your life you wrote only orders for cattle feed and barbwire…"

"Annie gave me this idea. She gave me all the papers and pictures belonging to the ranch from the old homestead and some books written by my brother Erik. He had talent, by the way. I never expected it. I loved those books. Annie suggested that I could write a history of this ranch and our family, as a historical book or as a fiction novel."

"Don't tell me you're not bored by this." Tristan said grabbing another sugar cookie.

"Bored? How can I be bored?" He leaned closer like imparting a big secret. "Writing is like a bug. Once you start, you're caught. I sit here, look outside to the vastness of this land and I feel inspired. Annie does the same, only she's dreaming of brave knights looking like Lance and all that romantic fluff. This…," he said slapping a hand over the printed papers on his desk, "…is going to be a serious, historical book," he said with so much pride that Tristan refrained from telling him that historical books are not in much demand these days.

The Old Man waved his hand. "Now, tell me about you. What brings you here?"

Tristan leaned forward in his chair and rested his elbows on his knees. "You didn't tell me the truth, at least not all the truth, last time we talked."

"What do you mean? I told you everything I knew." Maitland was the picture of honest indignation, only Tristan knew him better.

"I went to see all three men. I have sent to the lab DNA samples for two of them."

"Only two? One didn't want to give it?" The Old Man's eyes sparkled with interest.

"One was not necessary. Walter Dunn, after visiting prisons in various states for different lengths of time, settled as an antiques dealer in Cheyenne living in harmony with his partner."

"So?" Maitland's eyes widened. "You mean Walter Dunn is gay? I didn't know that."

"Also," Tristan continued, "he imparted an interesting piece of information. That Mama was very much in love with you. Now, why would he say this? I lived with you and Mama all my life and I can't say there was too much love spread around."

"Hmm, Dunn was mistaken."

"Maybe, he was. But then the second candidate to be my father told me the same. That Mama was in love with you. Who was mistaken and who was telling the truth? Would you care to give a DNA sample too, Old Man?"

Maitland looked at him straight. "I told you before, Tristan, I'd be proud to have fathered you, but I didn't." Tristan knew right then that the Old Man was not lying. He honestly believed what he was saying. "I will give a DNA sample for your peace of mind, but the truth is I don't know who your biological father is. Your mother always implied that I was, but I knew I was not. This was one of the matters of discord between us."

"I believe you. I have always felt that you are not my father probably because you were somewhat distant. But you treated Raul the same way, and

Lance worse."

The Old Man winced. "What else did Hartman say?"

"That you treated Mama with indifference. That he loved her very much and she didn't return his feelings."

"But she was intimate with him," Maitland pronounced with bitterness. "So much for love."

Tristan was somewhat embarrassed and reluctant to tell Maitland all the details. But he had to in order to get to the truth. "Only once. You rejected her and she ran to Hartman. In the morning, he asked her to marry him and she refused. End of story from his point of view."

"Hmm, that's why he left and never came back. I wondered."

Tristan fueled himself with another cookie before the last part of his story. "Hartman was a very nice man and I wouldn't mind him to be my father. Chances are he's not. The last one, Sean Kowalski, now that is a nasty man. A terror in his house, I wouldn't be surprised if he abuses his entire family. Wife and kids."

"Is he married?"

"Yes, he married latter in life and has six kids. Unlike the other two, he claimed Mama was in love with him..."

"What? No, she was not. The little twerp was following her, almost stalking her. She complained how annoying he was all the time."

"Yes, well, his memories are different. She was crazy about him and of course, he said, they had been intimate. In fact, Mama told him she was pregnant, but he could not marry her because of his career and mostly his religion, he being such a pious Catholic. So she had to marry you instead. Poor Katherine - his words."

"What a lying, miserable..."

"I agree and the idea that he might be my biological father makes me regret digging for the truth."

Maitland leaned back in his chair, closing his

eyes exhausted. "You'll let me know when the DNA results come back, won't you? It's an issue that ate at my sanity."

"Who my father was?"

"No. There was no doubt in my mind that I was your father, adopted or natural didn't matter. I never won Father of the Year Award, but I was your father...." He paused then continued in a barely audible voice, "It was her; Katherine sleeping around like my first wife did that bothered me."

CHAPTER 19

The lawyer recommended by TJ, Joanna Price, called them that evening and said that they needed to be present in court next morning at 10am for arbitration. Judge Parker was fair and she thought it was a clear case no problem.

Tristan fretted all evening and Eleanor tried to calm him down although she was worried a bit. Of course Tristan was the legal and de facto parent for Zach and arguments were overwhelmingly in his favor, and Eleanor's legal knowledge understood this, but being directly involved in this case gave her a shiver of apprehension. Only Zach was confident, in a child's simple way of regarding a situation - he'd go in front of the judge and say that he was not going with a woman he didn't know even if she claimed to be his mother.

They were in court early, waiting for their attorney, when Sanders, accompanied by two middle-aged men in suits, probably his highly-paid lawyers and a purple-dressed Norah came in. They occupied the seats on the other side of the aisle. Norah gave them a fulminating look from under the large hat she wore.

Zach was not paying her any attention, busy as he was to look behind to see who entered the room. And so they came and Zach waved at them grinning from ear to ear. Lance and Annie sitting right behind them, Raul with his mother, Carmelita, then Maitland with Pepe who was fussing around the Old Man. Then Lucky, Stork, and a few other ranch hands. Even Trish with her boyfriend, Tristan's associate in white coat, and a few patients scheduled for that morning. What did they do? Left the animals in kennels and closed the clinic?

Tristan turned and whispered, "Ellie, did you call them?"

Zach, whose ears caught the question, answered smiling. "I called Annie and she told the others."

Finally, TJ came in and with a booming voice

announced to the people outside, "No more space, folks. We'll let you know…" and he closed the door behind him.

Judge Conrad Parker, first cousin with rancher Parker, Maitland's neighbor, shuffled the papers in front of him. "So, we have an arbitration. Ms. Norah Sanders of Denver, Colorado has petitioned for full custody of the minor Zach Maitland of Laramie, Wyoming, age 9." He set his glasses on the desk and looked at the crowded room. "You know, in all my time on the bench I haven't seen so many people manifesting their interest in a criminal trial and this is only an arbitration." He shook his head in wonder. "Now, Ms. Sanders proceed with your petition."

One of the suited men rose and with a nasal tone started to plead the case. "Your Honor, my client, Ms. Norah Sanders, granddaughter of the distinguished Mr. Robert Sanders, gave birth to the child Zach Maitland when she was young, a mere twenty-one years old, in Denver Colorado. She was a student at University of Colorado at the time and she met the boy's father there. They were not married. Young love. For nine years she knew nothing of the boy. Now, she thinks that the child needs a mother's love and care and that they should be reunited. Of course, the Sanders family is very wealthy and they can ensure that the child has the best care and education in Denver. The prestige of Mr. Robert Sanders is well-known and it would be a clear advantage for the boy to live with the Sanders family."

"Hmm, Ms. Price, what do you have to say to this?"

Joanna Price rose smiling her benign grandmotherly smile. "I can understand Ms. Sanders' plight. She was twenty-one, student in college, unwed. What could she do? She signed away her parental rights and left the hospital as soon as she could."

"I was young and foolish," Norah cried.

"Yes, you were, my dear. Now, let's see, the

father was…ah, twenty-one, and a student and unwed. What did he do? He raised Zach as a single father, finished college, which you didn't Ms. Sanders, and went on to Veterinarian School, which he finished third in his class. Then he returned home to Laramie, where with the help of his family raised a fine, well-adjusted boy and built a veterinarian practice. To uproot the child from his home and family is unthinkable."

"A child needs his mother," Norah said.

"Of course. But are you that mother? Shall we discuss in detail what motivated your newly-found maternal instincts?"

Norah rose to blast her with another argument, when the judge intervened. "You made your point Ms. Price. Keep that thought in mind. For the moment, I would like to talk to the boy. Come here Zach. Not in front of me, here near me. I see a lot of people came here today."

"Yes, I told Annie and she let the others know," Zach smiled.

"And Annie is…," the judge prodded him.

Zach pointed with his finger. "She is right there with my Uncle Lance. They are recently wed so they hold hands and other mushy staff, you understand. Uncle Lance gave me Dolly."

"He gave you a doll?"

"No, Dolly is my white baby goat. She is so cute and afraid of the dark. I have to leave her a light on at night when I leave the barn and I still hear her crying. Everybody loves Dolly. Well, maybe not Carmelita after Dolly ate her brand new scarf."

"Carmelita is going to marry your father?"

Zach laughed. "No, Ellie is going to marry my father. You see right there holding on to my father's hand. She is a prosecutor in New York City."

"You don't say!" the judge exclaimed.

"Yes, and she wanted to be a judge, but don't worry she's not going to take your job. She needs to jump over the bar first," Zach said shrugging.

"To take the bar exam, you mean?"

"That's what I said. Carmelita is like a

grandmother to me. She is Uncle Raul's mother, there, in the second row. She bakes the most delicious chocolate chip cookies."

"I love chocolate chip cookies," the judge confessed.

Zach patted his hand. "She might give some to you too if you're good and do your chores. Everything she cooks is great. Sometimes I sneak some cookies to Toro."

"Another goat?"

"Toro is my little dog. Uncle Raul gave it to me."

Saunders' attorney rose. "I don't see how this is relevant to the case, Your Honor."

The judge inclined his head. "You'll see right away. How many animals do you have, Zach?"

"I have two horses, three dogs, two cats and the baby goat. But…" Zach came closer to the judge and told him in a conspiratorial tone, "…Uncle Raul showed me a little calf, rejected by his mama and I had to feed him milk with a bottle. He was so cute and you know what? Uncle Raul promised I could have him, if Dad agrees."

Tristan turned to Raul. "You didn't."

Raul only smiled showing his white teeth, amused by Tristan's dilemma, to increase his menagerie to please his son or to reject a poor, orphan calf.

"Ah," the judge said. "That's quite a lot of animals. Is there a place for them in Denver?"

"We can find a stable somewhere in the countryside to house them," Norah said dismissively.

"No way. My animals stay with me. I take care of them and talk to them daily. Besides I'm not going to stay with you in Denver," Zach argued frowning.

"Why is that?" the judge asked. "You don't like it there?"

Zach shrugged. "It's a big house, although kind of dark and gloomy. You know like where unhappy people live. But it doesn't matter. My home is here with Dad and Ellie and the animals and where the rest of my family lives. I have a science project to finish with my friend Jake, basketball and wrestling practice, to ride with Uncle Raul and to help Grandpa Maitland to write his book. I won't go. You can't make me."

"The child needs some discipline to listen to the adults in his family. It's not up to him where he will live," Norah said.

"You can't make me. I'll run away."

"As you see, Your Honor the child is unruly and disobedient without a mother to guide him."

"And how would you guide him Norah? At thirty years of age you have no steady job and live off your grandfather's fortune," Tristan intervened unable to keep quiet any longer.

People starting laughing and talking and Judge Parker knocked his gavel on the desk. "Quiet! Order in the room." Then he turned back to Zach. "How do you like your new mother-to-be, the prosecutor?"

"Oh, I like her very much. We clean the

kennels and stalls together. Ellie is cool," Zach said, smiling toward Eleanor, who was squirming in her chair wondering what to answer if asked when the wedding was to be? These people had jumped the gun with their assumptions.

"Very well." The judge rubbed his hands. "I find that the boy Zach Maitland has a wonderful family and great parents in the vet doctor and his future wife and it is ludicrous to imagine him living elsewhere. It would be detrimental to the child to tear him from the only place he can call home and from the father that has raised him since he was born."

Norah jumped up. "We'll appeal in Denver. Our family can offer him a wealthy life. We'll appeal."

"No." The single word said in a normal tone reverberated in the room and for a moment it was complete silence. "No," Sanders repeated.

"But, but…"Norah said confused. One look in her grandfather's eyes made her realize that he was serious and his decision final. With an exclamation of frustration, Norah ran from the room.

"Forgive an old man for entertaining thoughts of having a great-grandson with him in the last years of his life. It was selfish of me and it was never my intention to create havoc in Zach's life," Sanders said.

"Nonsense," Annie came to him dragging Lance after her. "He is still your great-grandson and you gained a big family, us. Come with us to the Circle M ranch where Carmelita has prepared a feast to celebrate."

The arbitration was over and the people talking about the events emptied the room.

"Maitland!" Judge Parker called the Old Man. "What is that book I hear you are writing?"

CHAPTER 20

The little dog on the examination table was trembling with fear. Slowly Tristan ran his hands over his small body. The dog looked at him with his small black button eyes from under shaggy hair and put out his tiny pink tongue, panted a few times then calmed down. The ordeal with vaccinations was forgotten.

"Doctor, you have magic touch. Baker would never let anyone touch him like that," pronounced the owner of the dog before exiting the room.

What people didn't know was that the touch, the contact with the animals was soothing for Tristan too.

The door opened again and Trish entered with a worried look on her face. "Tristan, come quick. There is a man in the kennels trying to give Poppy something to swallow. He didn't see me. Hurry!"

Poppy was their resident bulldog, left on their doorstep abandoned by his owner. Tristan nursed him to health and now was trying to find a family to adopt him. Poppy was very fussy with his food and no stranger could make him eat what he didn't like and he was very particular in his taste.

They ran to the annex that housed the animals and Tristan saw a man shaking the bulldog's jowls in frustration. He grabbed the man by the collar and turning him around pushed him against the wall.

"What do you know? An old acquaintance, Mr. Jody Coates."

"Do you know him, Tristan?" asked Trish frowning at a Ziploc bag she found in the dog's kennel. Poppy the bulldog, escaped from the clutches of the man intent to force him to swallow something that didn't agree with him, gave a loud howl of complaint.

"Yeah, he's pestering Marybeth. This time I'm calling the police."

"Whatever for?" Coates protested. "I ain't done nothing."

"Do you have any idea what this is?" Trish

asked Tristan giving him the small plastic bag.

Tristan looked at it, sniffed carefully and nodded. "My guess is, this is rat poison. He wanted to poison our animals."

"But why?"

Coates tried to slink along the wall and escape toward the exit. Tristan grabbed him and pushed him in an empty stall. Then he got a lock and fixed it to the door, locking a protesting Coates inside.

"But why" Trish asked again baffled. "Why would he poison our animals?"

"Who knows how his twisted mind works? To file a complaint with the Humane Society against us that we kill animals or to make trouble for Marybeth because she's taking care of the animals in the annex. Who knows? Go and call the police, Trish."

"Don't do that or Marybeth will suffer," Coates threatened.

"I warned you. Come again and I call the

police for unlawful entering in a private place, for assaulting my personnel and trying to poison my animals."

Trish ran out to make the call just when Marybeth entered. When she saw Coates locked in the stall she paled. "Jody what have you done? I gave you all the money I had," she wailed.

"It ain't enough. I need more," he answered sullenly. "Tell your boss here to let me out and not to call the police."

Marybeth turned imploring eyes to Tristan. "Please, Tristan. He can destroy me."

For the first time, Tristan wanted to shake her for her dramatic approach to every situation. "Come with me, please," he said guiding her to his office.

He closed the door, gave the sniffling Marybeth a tissue and led her to his chair behind the desk.

"Now, Marybeth, you are going to talk to me and answer my questions. Not because I'm your employer, your private life is your own...." Tristan paused reflecting on today's events. "…although, you being involved in any way with a person who attempts to poison my animals, makes it my business. I want you to tell me the truth as an old time friend and as Raul's brother."

"I can't…" Fresh tears flooded Marybeth eyes and Tristan thanked heaven that Eleanor was such a well-tempered reasonable woman, not prone to hysterics. Marybeth suffered from depression and she needed counseling.

"Listen Marybeth, first you have my promise that whatever you chose to tell me will remain between the two of us. I am good at keeping secrets. Lord knows I have a bunch of my own, who doesn't? I don't gossip. Make me understand what demons torment you so."

She raised her teary eyes to him. "I made mistakes."

"We all did. We are humans. No one should suffer like you do. How can you, an intelligent woman, let that low-life, Jody Coates, have so much power over you and blackmail you?"

"He… he can harm someone I love," she confessed after a short hesitation.

"Raul? He can take care of himself. You should trust him."

She shook her head, obscuring her scar with her hair as she usually did. "No, not Raul."

"Does Raul know the truth?"

"Somewhat. Not entirely."

Tristan gave her another tissue. "All right, tell me. You have to talk to someone. It might as well be me."

Marybeth wiped her tears and looked at him. "When I was in high school I was very lonely. Nobody wanted to be friends with me, not even my sisters. To be honest, I was resentful for their part in my accident and whatever feeble attempts at being closer they made, I rejected them and shied away."

"Oh, Marybeth, for so long I held myself guilty for challenging Lance to ride the wild mustang, until we made peace and came to terms with the reality. I was a kid, he was a bit reckless, and Barnett wanted to harm him. Very unfortunate, but it's time to move on."

"Do you think he has moved on?" she asked.

"Absolutely. Lance is so happy and so much in love, he floats on air. Annie has this effect on people. She spreads love. Even Maitland, gruff as he is listens to Annie like she was the Oracle of Delphi."

Marybeth smiled through tears. "Yeah. She is something. At my parents anniversary party, she came with a beer bottle to defend me against an aggressive, drunk cowboy."

Tristan laughed. "I didn't know that. What happened?"

"Raul scared him off. But Annie was terrific."

"So you see, it's enough to have the love and support of one person and what others believe cease to matter. You can be happy too."

She shook her head in denial. "Not me. Jody Coates approached me when I was in high school. He was older, twenty-three to my fifteen and while I was

232

cautious at the beginning, he was so charming – he can be when he wants, you know – that slowly I warmed up to him and opened up to his friendship."

"I understand. Every girl wants to have a boyfriend."

"Not me. Besides it was all a secret and nobody knew about this. We both agreed that it was better this way. This was my mistake, to trust him."

An ugly thought crossed Tristan's mind. "Marybeth, were you raped?"

After a longer hesitation, she answered. "Not really. He was pressuring me for quite some time to have sex and I kept refusing. One afternoon when we drove farther in his truck, he became more persistent and angry at me for saying no. And in the end I stopped protesting or pushing him away. It was a horrible experience and after that I avoided him."

"I still think it was rape if you said no and he persisted."

"No, no. It was my fault for agreeing to see him, for keeping company with him." She halted, lost in thoughts. "After a while I discovered that I was pregnant."

"What?"

She nodded. "Nobody knew about this. I told Jody and this was when he left town. I dropped out of school and went to stay with an aunt in Reno, Nevada. She arranged with a couple to adopt the child. It was a healthy baby boy and the minute I gave birth to him I loved him more than anyone else in the world. He was mine. But I was sixteen, without a job or skills of any kind, so my aunt convinced me that the best for him would be to give him up for adoption. It was a private arrangement. I promised them not to interfere in their lives ever and they promised that they will send me pictures and news about him every year on his birthday."

"The things we do for love, misguided decisions and pointless sacrifices," Tristan commented.

"Why do you say that?"

"That's my opinion. If you brought him on

the ranch and raised him yourself, he might have been a happy, healthy child. We'll never know. I understand you were sixteen and scared, though."

"This is not it. I had no job to support us both and Papa was adamant that he wants no bastard in his family. Where was I to go?"

Tristan patted her hand to comfort her. "I'm sorry, Marybeth. I had no right to judge. You have been in an impossible situation."

"Impossible it is now. Jody came back and he is desperate for money. I gave him what I had, but at some point he grabbed my purse and searched it. He found the pictures and address and all." She bent her head trying to stop the tears threatening to overflow. "He doesn't care it's his child he'll harm. He wants to go and bully that family into giving him money or he'll sue for his paternity rights. He can do it. Technically, he didn't sign the adoption papers. That family is not very rich and the mother was sick lately and she had medical tests done and they don't need this complication added to their problems. Jody is my mess to deal with, not theirs."

"I see."

"That's why I'm trying to hold off Jody the best I can. I'll borrow money if I have to. You see now, Tristan why we have to let him go and not involve the police."

"Don't you know that a blackmailer will not back off? No matter how much you give him, he'll come back again and again. Tell you what we'll do. The police will take him away and Judge Parker will put him in jail for all his misdeeds."

"No. He'll talk and he'll harm the boy." Marybeth was frightened.

"Listen, you have to face your fears or you'll have no life. The past is what it is and we can't change it. Nobody's perfect and we all make mistakes. Don't run away any longer, Marybeth. He'll talk, maybe people will talk and it will be an eighth day wonder. Then we'll go on with our life."

"The boy will be hurt."

Tristan realized with sadness that it was the

boy she was concerned about, but not Raul being hurt. His big brother was up for a lot of heartache. "Chances are the boy knows he had been adopted. If not, at his age - I suppose he's about Zach's age - it's high time he knew the truth."

"The family doesn't want him to know he was adopted."

"That's too bad. It's okay to protect the children when they are small, but later on, when they have a better understanding, they should be told the truth. Not doing so can be a source of mistrust and unhappiness." He patted her hand again. "All will be well you'll see. You'll feel so relieved to get rid of Coates for good, not to be a victim any longer, and not to let him have power over you and over your life. And please, Marybeth, if you don't care for Raul, don't string him along. Just tell him so. He is a decent guy who deserves to be happy too."

The police car sirens could be heard louder and louder.

CHAPTER 21

The Old Man had fallen asleep in his comfortable chair in front of the window overlooking his ranch and the vast Wyoming prairie. He was dreaming of times long gone and people who faced adversities to settle this land.

A knock on the door awoke him. Tristan came in and snatching one of Carmelita's cookies from the platter took a seat in the chair nearby. Mmm, good! Oatmeal raisins cookies with sugar icing this time. He remembered that when he was a kid he used to lick the sweet glaze first then bite in the soft cookie, warm from the rack.

"Hey Tristan!" Maitland said, startled from his deep slumber. "What is the matter. I hope you don't have more trouble from your ex-wife?"

"She was not my wife, heaven forbid. I was young and naïve but not that stupid to marry Norah."

"Yes, you young people do everything backwards. First bring kids in to the world, then marry, and by the time you're ready to fall in love, you do it with someone other then the spouse. And then you divorce," the Old Man grumbled.

"Your generation was no better and I'm the living proof," Tristan replied.

"Did you find out anything?"

Tristan got up and started pacing the room. "As a matter of fact I did. I got the DNA results from the lab."

"And...who was your father?"

"You seem inordinately interested in this subject," Tristan commented, then turned on his heel to face Maitland. "You are interested. You sent me on this entire witch hunt for your own purposes."

"You wanted to know who your father is, so I gave you whatever information I had. But yes, I wanted to know. You see Katherine had always claimed that I was the only one she had been intimate with. Oh, she had suitors aplenty, vying for her attention, but she claimed that she had always been faithful to me. And yet I knew you were not my son, so I knew she lied. That's why I could never trust her."

"Mama lied all the time, what's new?"

"She asked me to trust her and I could not. I guess now that we are separated, I want that confirmation. I want to know with whom she had been unfaithful."

Tristan shrugged. The Old Man's thinking was a bit muddled. "What does it matter? She was unfaithful with Cole Warner for years. Did you care?"

"No. I mean no man would like to be cuckolded, but I didn't care enough to prevent it. That's what she said when she left me. However, then, before you were born, it mattered. I was still hurting after my first wife's betrayal and I wanted Katherine to be true. When I realized she betrayed me too, I considered that it's just as well. I couldn't trust any woman. First I left her, then I came back, and we continued our relationship. Four years later when I asked her to marry me, I told her that I will never love her or trust her."

"And she accepted."

Maitland inclined his head. "Yes, she did. Her life was not easy and I think she hoped to change my mind, not to mention to convince me you were my son. Now, tell me what have you find out."

"Good news for me is that, that obnoxious person, Sean Kowalski, is not my father." Tristan resumed his pacing.

"Pshaw! Of course not. He was the one pestering your mother, not the other way around. Besides he was too poor for your mother to consider him seriously. Katherine is a very complex and complicated person, and sometimes I wondered if she knew what drove her to act in some way or another."

Tristan took another cookie and sat back in the chair. He licked the sugar icing first, remembering how Carmelita used to bake cookies especially for him and how possessively his mother tried to keep him apart from her. "When I was a kid Mama was my only anchor in the world. Then I started to realize that either she was misguided or she had her own purposes and I was only a pawn. All my dreams of having a loving mother came to a halt when she pushed me to goad Lance to ride the wild mustang. She knew that Shorty Barnett had placed a burr under the saddle. She knew what would happen and she left me to agonize with guilt for years. I had nightmares long after and I was wary of her after that."

Maitland was remembering that unfortunate day in vivid details too. "It was not so simple. Lance was a young buck, hotheaded and reckless and most of the fault is his for trying to ride the wild mustang. Now, tell me about the DNA results."

"Yes. I guess I could be happy. No gambler, frequent prison visitor, nor pious, child abuser. Hartman is a decent, genuinely nice fellow. It would be good to know I have good genes. He is also rich and bent to leave me his fortune."

"So, what's wrong with this picture?"

"Nothing is wrong. Only here is the

interesting news. Hartman is not my father. The DNA test is categorical, no match."

Maitland blinked as if awaken from slumber. "What? No match?"

"Nope. Now you tell me why you were so convinced all your life that I am not your son. And if not you, who else could be?"

"There was no one else or maybe a one night stand. How should I know?"

"Old Man, you're grasping at straws. All my life you told me that I'm not your son. Why?"

"Because I believed so." Maitland struck the desk with his hand. His useful, handy whip had long been confiscated by Annie. "Because Katherine never came to say straight that you are my son. She was never firm. She implied only that you might be my son, that of course you are, she said in such a way that everyone doubted it. Remember?"

Tristan raked his hair with his fingers and grabbed another cookie. "Yes, I remember. It made no sense especially because her main purpose in life was to establish me as the rightful heir of the ranch. She could have lied more convincingly, if she wanted…. Unless, in a way, she didn't believed it herself. Yes, that must be it. Ha! Mama thought that I was Hartman's son. Isn't that an irony? She thought that because of that one night spent with Hartman, I'm his son."

Maitland looked at him like seeing him for the first time. "Sometimes I let myself believe that you are indeed mine, only to remember women are treacherous and shake that thought away. How about you Tristan? You also said you felt I was not your father."

"I think it had to do with your aloofness. I was a kid and my two brothers rejected me and I wanted a father. You had never been affectionate or communicative. I resented that. Of course you treated Raul and Lance the same if not worse. But at the time I didn't compare. I just resented you for keeping me at a distance. And, as you said Mama was not very convincing that I was your son, so everybody tacitly agreed that I was not."

"Do you want a DNA sample from me?" Maitland asked a world of hope in his voice.

Tristan rose, placed back on the platter the cookie he had just grabbed and came closer to the window and the Old Man's chair. He placed one hand on his shoulder, while looking outside to the ranch where he'd grown up and to the vast space beyond. A feeling of belonging to this place, this family, with this people, flooded him like never before.

"No," he finally said. "I'm done with DNA testing. Ellie made me realize the reason I don't feel any connection with Hartman, who was such a decent and worthy fellow I'd have been proud to call father." Maitland winced under his hand. "The reason why I didn't feel any vibes for any of them was because they were strangers. Regardless of the DNA results, they were never a part of my life. I don't need any more tests because as far as I'm concerned, aloof or not, you have been here for me always. You shouted at me and cracked your whip to get back on the saddle after the spirited horse threw me for the first time…"

Maitland frowned. "I don't recall that. Has a horse, any horse ever thrown you?"

"Yes. When I was ten and Shorty brought another wild mustang. I suppose I wanted to prove something or I wanted to punish myself for what I did to Lance. I don't know. I was pretty shook up and dazed. When you got out of the house and yelled at me to get back on the horse, I considered you cruel at the time. Now I know better. You did the only thing possible for me to ride again and not fear the horses. You forced me to face my fears and get rid of them."

"You became an expert rider. Better than Lance, who is a rodeo champion."

"Not better, but good. Can you picture a vet, fearing to approach horses?"

"They say you are a horse whisperer, a magician. They say that you can talk any wild beast into listening and obeying you."

"Nah, I'm just a good vet. I love animals and they feel it. Again, when I was a kid and all the ranch hands were laughing that I befriended wild animals and ornery bulls and cattle, you were the only one who encouraged me and never mocked me. Later on, you supported my dreams to go to vet school and open the practice in Laramie."

"Hmm!" Maitland mumbled deep in thoughts.

"You were there, at all my graduation ceremonies. Your presence was with me even when you were not there in person. When Zach was born…"

The Old Man smiled. "I remember you called us at midnight to tell us we have a grandchild. Your Mama had her face covered with a greenish muck. She said it kept her skin younger."

"You encouraged me to bring him home at the ranch, to be raised here."

"But you did not."

"You made it possible for me to hire a nanny and go to college and vet school."

247

"That's what you wanted."

"Yes. What you don't know is that Norah had pressured me to give him up for adoption and while I never considered it, sometimes I wondered if I was doing the right thing for Zach or I was just selfish to want him with me. Thanks to your encouragement and support it all worked out well."

"Yes well." The Old Man coughed to cover his emotion.

"So you see, from my point of view I don't need a DNA test anymore to tell me who my father is. When all is said and done, I have only one real father and that one is you."

CHAPTER 22

The days were inching slowly one into the other and it was already mid-August. The last days of summer were quite warm, but at night there was a chill in the air, a sign of the approaching fall.

That Friday night, Tristan came home late and quite tired after a long operation on a sheep dog that got into trouble with a wild animal, probably a coyote. Tristan was looking forward to a nice dinner with his family. Eleanor had visited the Circle M ranch and Carmelita had sent a large casserole of her chicken enchiladas. Yummy! And then, after they tucked Zach into bed, he anticipated their late night talk on the porch looking at the stars and the moon as a nice reward after a long workday.

They were seated all three of them at the large table in the kitchen, savoring the enchiladas when a knock on the front door startled them all.

"Who could it be at this hour?" Eleanor asked.

Tristan shrugged and pushing his plate aside rose to open the door. "A doctor is always on call for emergencies. If there is a sick animal, I have to go."

He opened the door and his mother, very elegant and radiant, entered without waiting for an invitation.

"Tristan darling!" she exclaimed, kissing him on both cheeks, in French style.

"Nana!" Zach cried, coming to embrace his grandmother. He wrinkled his nose. "What is that smell?" he asked.

"This is Chanel no.5, dear," she said affectionately, kissing him too. "The most refined and sophisticated of the French perfumes," she explained patting his cheek.

"Please come eat with us," Eleanor invited in her most polite tone.

Relieved of her jacket, Katherine Maitland took a seat at the table. "No thank you," she said covering her empty plate with her hand, when Eleanor wanted to place some enchiladas on her plate. "My delicate stomach doesn't agree with the Mexican food, especially the spicy one cooked by Carmelita and I see her signature in this."

Eleanor looked at Tristan not knowing what else to serve her. "Maybe some cookies. I bought them in town," she added for reassurance.

"No, dear, thank you. Please sit down and continue your dinner. I'm only going to tell Tristan my news and I'll be gone. I'm staying at the hotel in town," Katherine said smiling at Eleanor. "By the way, I like you much better than your younger sister, the one that married Lance." She nodded with satisfaction.

"I'm the youngest, ma'am. Annie is the middle sister. She is much shorter than me; maybe that's why she seems younger."

"Shorter, yes. Impertinent too. And that hair…" Katherine shuddered in horror. "Anyhow she's good for Lance. They fit together.…You however, are a beauty. And such refined manners. I approve wholeheartedly of my son's choice. I hope you'll invite me to the wedding."

"Mother, you're jumping the gun," Tristan stopped her, not knowing if to laugh or whisk his mother away before she said something more outrageous.

"What? You haven't asked her yet? What are you waiting for? Don't tell me it's too soon. She's living here, isn't she?"

Zach looking from one adult to the other added his comment. "Ellie is a prosecutor in New York City, but she will marry my Dad, aren't you?" he asked, a note of incertitude in his voice.

"I have to settle some issues in New York, and then I'll be free to make decisions, Zach. And I love you too. Don't doubt that ever," Eleanor said looking at Zach fondly.

Tristan saw the need to change the subject. Eleanor knew his feelings and she should not be pressured. "So mother, what brings you to Laramie?"

Katherine turned to him eager to impart her news. "Tristan, I wanted to tell you that I am so grateful to you. Two of my most beloved friends from my youth called me. Walter Dunn, ah, we had so much fun together and I was so happy to hear his voice. And dear, dear Edgar, the love of my life. How on earth did you guess he is your real father?" Tristan opened his mouth to correct her, but she continued. "When I was at my lowest, poor and abandoned in Denver, he came like a knight on a white charger, - he has a white Lincoln SUV, you know – and he rescued me and made my life bright again," she finished with a dramatic flair.

"What can I say? I'm glad to hear…," Tristan said looking with regret at the congealed enchiladas on his plate. Without a word, Eleanor rose and taking his plate placed it in the microwave to warm it up.

"We are going to be married in Jackson and you are all invited." Katherine beamed at them all.

"What? But you are married to father…," Tristan protested, feeling a headache coming in force.

"Bah!" Katherine waved her hand dismissing the argument. "I've been to the ranch and talked to

Maitland. I filed for divorce and it will be very fast. He owes it to me after so many years of unhappiness. And don't call him 'Father'."

"Maitland is my father. He adopted me and raised me, supporting my career and dreams. Besides all my life you told me and everyone else around that he is my father."

"What was I to do?" Katherine argued. "I had to give you a home, a name and I hoped, the ranch." She balled her fists. "But you had to prefer to care for dirty animals instead. If you'd been more interested, Maitland might have left the ranch to you."

"What did Maitland say about the divorce?" Tristan inquired.

"He agreed. He is a doddering old fool. He was interested only in some stupid book he's writing. Like anybody will want to read stories about long dead people and their life before civilization came to these parts."

"The fact is that he is at least ten years younger than Hartman," Tristan pointed out.

"Yes, yes. But he is not as vigorous and active as Hartman. Besides, if Edgar dies, I'll be a rich widow and this time, I'll make sure it's all clear in the will. No more threat of poverty for me." She sighed with satisfaction and rose to go. "I have to go now, darlings."

"Mother, I happen to like this guy, Hartman, very much. He is a decent fellow. What I want to say is - I feel responsible that I created this entire situation. If you make him unhappy or take advantage of his kindness to hurt him, I'll be very, very upset."

Katherine kissed him on the cheek. "Don't worry darling. I promise you I'll make him very happy. I already did. I love him, you see. Thirty years ago I was a silly girl chasing the moon and I didn't realize what a treasure he was. But that is water under the bridge. Try not to make the mistakes I did. Good bye."

After she left, they finished eating in silence.

"I feel like I opened a can of worms with my

inquiry. Hartman will suffer," Tristan said at last.

Eleanor closed the dishwasher's door with a snap. "You know, I'm not so sure. I don't know your mother well, but the only other time I saw her was when Maitland told us of his wishes and she was upset, bitter, distraught even. Now she was radiant and content."

"She was distraught that Maitland didn't leave her any money."

"She was distraught that by not leaving her anything, Maitland proved again that he didn't love or appreciate her," Eleanor corrected him.

"I have to talk to Hartman," Tristan said.

"Yes, you do," Eleanor agreed. "To tell him about the DNA results. It's only right to inform him."

Tristan went to his office and called Edgar Hartman. He answered immediately.

"Hartman here."

"Hi. This is Tristan Maitland."

"Tristan, it's good of you to call. Your mother told me so many things about you."

"Yes, well. She was here and that's what I wanted to talk to you about," Tristan said.

"You disapprove of her living with me," he heard Hartman's worried voice.

"No, no, Edgar. That's not it. Besides I could disapprove till doomsday and my mother would do what she pleases." Tristan hastened to reassure the older man. "You see, I created this whole situation with my inquiry and I feel responsible. My mother grew to be a very hard and self-centered woman. I'm afraid she'll take advantage of you."

"You worry for me?" Hartman laughed. "That is so nice. Thank you. Nobody has worried for me in a long time, if ever. Let me explain to you a few things. I am seventy-seven years old, but I am not senile. My mind is still sharp. I had to work hard and fight for all I had in my life. Frankly, you don't make a fortune by being a naïve fool."

"I didn't say that." Tristan protested. "I said you are too decent and my mother might take advantage."

"What? You think she wants my money. She can have it. I am not going to take my money with me to heaven. Besides, I have enough wealth to spend in three lifetimes. Katherine is welcome to it. What you don't understand is that I can give her more than money. I can give her love. Every day I tell her how much I love her and she absorbs it like a flower without any water for too long. Katherine needs love and approval constantly. I give it to her honestly and with an open heart. We are too old to play games and the time left is precious." His voice wobbled a bit.

"Ellie said something similar," Tristan muttered.

"What I'm going to tell you will surprise you even more. Katherine loves me back. For various reasons. First, it was gratitude. She was bored in Denver and alone. Then she opened her heart a little more every day. I make her happy, you see. Maitland didn't and he did not love her. She hid her love for him until it withered and died. It came as a surprise to her that I don't hide my feelings and I tell her all the time how much I adore her. It is my pleasure to spoil her, indulging her every whim."

"I can't picture her this way," Tristan blurted.

"Because she was never happy or even content. I thank the good Lord every day for bringing her into my life. Now, did you get the DNA results?"

"Ah yes. About that, Edgar, I consider you one of the nicest men I met and I would have been happy and proud to have your genes. Unfortunately, the results were negative."

There was a pause like the other one tried to absorb this news. "I confess I hoped despite the slim chances, that you are my son. Katherine is convinced that you are." Pause again. "Anyhow, you are her son and perhaps you'll come see us and bring Zach and the young lady too, if it's not too much imposition."

"Of course we'll come. Zach likes you very much and so do I. We'll keep in touch and visit often, I promise. Take care of yourself, Edgar. Bye."

Eleanor had come into the office and caressed

his cheek. "He loves her. Are you now realizing that she loves him in return? Not the same kind of adoration he has for her, but she cares too and I bet she will take care of him with devotion."

"Devotion? My mother?"

"Yes. Without him, who would adore her like that?"

CHAPTER 23

It was past midnight.

"Ellie, psst, Ellie!"

"What? What?" Eleanor woke up and looked at Tristan raised on his elbow above her. "Did you have a nightmare?"

"Yes. I dreamt that I was losing you."

She placed her hand on his stubbly jaw. "Silly. You will never lose me. Don't you know that?"

"No, I don't. You have never said so. Prove it."

"Okay. Tomorrow…"

" No, now," he said urgency in his tone.

She smiled. "Insatiable. You want to make love again."

"No. Marry me."

"O-okay. Tomorrow…"

He shook his head. "Now. Eleanor Jackson, will you marry me?"

She pushed her hair from her face. He was dead serious and it was the middle of the night. "Yes Tristan. Tonight, tomorrow, whenever you want I will marry you. Now can we go back to sleep?"

He gathered her closer to him. "Tonight. I Tristan McNamara Maitland take you Eleanor Jackson to be my lawfully wedded wife because I love you and I can't live without you. I promise to be faithful, how could I not? To love and cherish you all my life, for rich or poor, in sickness or health, forever." He placed a ring on her finger. It was too dark for Eleanor to see it, but it fit. "Now you."

He was so sweet, she had to indulge him in this fantasy and it was endearing. "I Eleanor Delphine Jackson take you Tristan Maitland to be my lawfully husband because I find you to be the sexiest man on earth and the best lover a girl can dream of." He tickled her. "To love and cherish you, and perhaps obey you sometimes when you make sense. Anything else? In sickness and in health for rich and I guarantee you, we'll not be poor. I'll love you forever. Amen." She finished, trying to see her ring in the dark.

"Ellie! Did you mean it?"

"Yes. Of course I meant it. Every word."

"Good," he said breathing deeply with relief. "Tomorrow we go to see Judge Parker and make it legal."

"Tomorrow?"

"Yes, tomorrow. Didn't you say so? Now you take it back?"

"No I don't," she said. "Our parents will kill us."

"You know we are adults and have been for quite some time. Although it's nice to have it, we don't need their approval." Tristan mumbled kissing her neck.

"What I wanted to…mm…point out… is that they wanted to give us a big wedding." She inclined her head to give him a better access.

"We'll have a big wedding with a pastor and all the trimmings later. Tomorrow however we'll make it legal in front of the judge. Any other objections?"

"Mm…" She might have had, but for the life of her she could not remember what, when he was kissing her like that.

Two days later, another bell ring at the front door interrupted their dinner.

"It's becoming a habit for people to come to visit us without calling first," Tristan mumbled while Eleanor went to open the door.

"James!" she exclaimed.

"Bathroom…," the newcomer croaked.

"Second door, on the right." Eleanor pointed down the hallway and turned to embrace her mother who came in after James.

"Darling, it seems James' delicate constitution didn't take well to the commuter flight from Denver to Laramie. I had to stop the rental car ten times on the way from the airport here. As for me, I got accustomed."

"Mama come sit with us. Why didn't you call to warn me you are coming and bringing James with you?" Eleanor asked placing some pot roast and mashed potatoes on a plate in front of her mother.

"For me it was a decision I made on the spur of the moment. Dear James, hearing you were coming back to New York City soon, wanted to surprise you, I think," her mother said, indulging in the food with great appetite, forgetting her calorie counting.

Eleanor made a face at Tristan and resumed eating too. "About my coming back soon, there might be a change in plans…"

James returned, a little pale, but looking much better. Tristan measured him up and down. Even ailing, James was a splendid looking man, like a blond Pierce Brosnan in his younger James Bond days. Tall, with golden hair and blue eyes, square jaw, well built, athletic body, not an inch of fat on him. How could Tristan compare with him in Eleanor's eyes?

James was sizing him up too. With a smile that unveiled perfect white teeth, James held out his hand. "Hi, I'm James Mason, Eleanor's fiancé."

Tristan shook his hand with equal strength. "I'm Tristan Maitland, Eleanor's husband."

Shouts of surprise, Zach's laughter, and the two little dogs barking created a lot of noise. When all quieted down a little, Eleanor's mother looked at her with exasperation. "Tell me it's not true and you didn't cheat me out of a giving you a nice wedding."

James was more dramatic. "Eleanor, how could you do this to me? I thought this was a vacation in the country side, your way of evading the reality."

"Everybody!…" Eleanor clapped her hands to get their attention. "Please sit down. I have some things to say. I'm thirty-three years old and I decide what course my life will take. James, in case your memory left you, I am not your fiancée, remember? You told me that if I don't comply with your wishes, our engagement was off and I gave you your ring back. Our wedding plans were canceled and I gladly compensated Mama for the loss."

"Yes, but, but I thought you'll come to your senses," he sputtered in protest.

Eleanor sighed. "Did you think that a prosecutor can be so weak-willed to be twisted around your finger? You didn't know me well and this says a lot about our relationship. Think what a lucky escape you had."

"I thought we had a good thing going. We are both so good-looking together. You are calm and level-headed. Father approves of you...Our nights together were great." James almost snarled provocatively at Tristan.

Tristan rose from his chair. Eleanor intervened between them. "Enough both of you. This was in the past," she said pushing Tristan back in his chair. Then turned to James. "What you said it's true, but there was one very important thing missing, love." She raised her hand when he wanted to protest. "Love and affection and deep respect for one another and loyalty. That's why you could so easily get involved with Margo."

"How can you accuse me of …"

"I don't accuse you. I only state the facts. And yes, for the same reasons, I didn't care and my heart was not involved and I was free to fall in love with a handsome, smart, perfect man for me," she said looking at Tristan.

"You'll be sorry, but it will be too late," James predicted in a somber tone.

"I won't. I thought this through all summer long. By the way, I resigned from my job as district attorney and I applied to take the Wyoming bar exam." Then Eleanor turned to face her mother, who was slumped in her chair. "Mama, this was not an overnight decision. I met Tristan in April, almost five months ago. I lived with him and Zach, mostly to supervise Zach with his summer activities, but also for myself. I felt relaxed and happy during this vacation and I realized that I could live like this forever. Tristan is the most handsome, hard-working, caring man I know. Above all, he makes me happy. Don't you want me to be happy?"

"Ah, Eleanor, of course I want you to be happy," her mother said, with tears in her eyes.

"I could have made you happier. Father wanted to gift us with the house in the Hamptons. And you preferred this," James said waving his hand derisively.

Eleanor shrugged. "To each his own, James. I don't want a house in the Hamptons. This vast open land and this man is what I want."

"What did Maitland say about not having a proper wedding?" her mother asked.

"About that...he didn't say a thing. He doesn't know we are married. But, please let me explain. Tristan and I, we decided to get married now and we did. Yesterday, in front of Judge Parker. However, if you guys want to have a large shindig, we can repeat our vows in front of a pastor later."

"A Christmas wedding." Eleanor's mother's eyes sparkled. "I have always thought a Christmas wedding is the most romantic of all. Brides prefer June because flowers are more bountiful then, but Christmas is the most magic time of year."

And so, one parent was content to have plenty of time to organize a grand social event. Telling Maitland was almost anticlimactic. He raised his eyes from the documents he was studying and said only, "Married? Ha, it was about time. If you had dithered some more, boy, the fancy New Yorker, James Something would have whisked her away."

CHAPTER 24

It was Friday after Thanksgiving and the Maitland family was gathered in the large family room at the Circle M ranch and was decorating a big Christmas tree. Everything needed to be perfect for the upcoming wedding ceremony that Pastor Gregory would officiate on Christmas day.

The family was replete with the good food that Carmelita had cooked for a week before Thanksgiving. Zach was playing with the dogs on the rug in front of the fireplace where a fire burned merrily and a barn cat had gotten inside and was batting at an ornament from the lower branch. Warm cider and cookies were continuously replenished by Carmelita and merry Christmas songs were played on the loudspeakers.

"I'll be home for Christmas..." Annie sang at the top of her voice and in complete disaccord with Bing Crosby. Lance looked at her with so much love and admiration, Maitland had to secretly brush a tear from his eyes.

The Old Man seated in a comfortable armchair was supervising the decoration. His writing and the extensive research he did about the local history made him do a genealogical study and a family tree. It needed to be as accurate as possible so in the end, Tristan submitted DNA tests to the lab. The results came back confirming without a doubt that Tristan was Maitland's biological son. Not that either of them had a doubt it would be so.

Elliott Maitland was very pleased to see all his family together and his three sons having fun. The two New York girls had worked miracles. Maitland was very happy with his two daughters-in-law. Annie with her bubbly personality and warm smile hid a steely determination to be admired. She was a blessing for Lance.

Beautiful, calm Eleanor, so different from Annie, was perfect for Tristan and Zach. Not too mention the heated way Eleanor and Tristan looked at each other across a crowded room could scorch the tablecloth. Yes, his two sons had chosen well and he was pleased. Now if Raul could stop dithering and choose a bride too, it would make his happiness complete. Unfortunately, Maitland didn't think Marybeth Parker was the right choice or that she could make Raul happy. He had promised himself not to interfere and he'd keep his promise. This didn't stop him from being worried though.

"Tristan, move that ornament a little higher to the right," Maitland instructed. "There is an empty spot there."

"Where did you see the empty spot?" Lance muttered. "The tree is so overloaded with ornaments it may collapse soon."

Maitland continued unfazed. "Raul, the angel top is crooked. Could you straighten it up, please?" Raul obeyed. "Yes, like that is better. Can we plug the lights in to see if all work? You know some bulbs could be burnt."

Eleanor had seen an empty spot on a brunch and bent down to hook a little glass bird there. In doing so she rubbed against Tristan who was replacing a spent bulb in the lights string. He gave her a smoldering look that accompanied by a wicked smile, promised a very satisfactory for both, retaliation.

Just then Lucky, the foreman, entered the room. He stopped to grab a glass with cider, kissed Carmelita's cheek and snatched a cookie too. Then he went to Raul and whispered some words in a voice so low nobody heard. Raul sobered and without a word exited the room in a hurry. Lucky, lingering a bit to admire the ornaments on the tree, followed him.

Tristan looked at Lance, raising an eyebrow questioningly. If there was trouble maybe they should go too.

Annie came closer to Lance and told him, "Go to see what's going on." She took the second string of lights from his hand. Lance kissed her mouth quickly and left.

Eleanor nodded to Tristan and he followed

Lance out.

They were on the front porch when they saw Marybeth Parker running out of the barn to her truck.

"Marybeth, wait," Tristan shouted, but she climbed in, fired the engine and drove away.

When they entered the barn they saw Raul seating on a bale of hay in a slumped, dejected posture. He raised anguished eyes at them, containing a world of pain and despair. "She left me. She is going to marry a man from Nevada."

Tristan came closer and placed his hand gently on Raul's shoulder. "She has a lot of problems..."

Raul turned to him. "If you want to say she is crazy..."

"No, no. She is troubled, I told you that before. It had all started with her accident when she was a girl."

"Yes I remember. She fell from her horse," Lance said.

Tristan shook his head. "The Parkers didn't

talk about this at all, but it was a fight between the sisters. Faith was the eldest, beautiful and spoiled and accustomed to have her way. The middle sister Dora, a washed out copy of the eldest was following Faith. Marybeth was different, pretty in her own way and aloof. The spat happened in the barn. Marybeth was currying her horse when Faith startled her and the horse with a loud banging. The horse pulled back and hit a rack with some farm tools, a rake, a shovel and a fork that fell down. Marybeth tripped over them and fell. She hit her head and cut her cheek. After that she became even more aloof and somehow obsessed that she is fated to be unlucky and unhappy. I think she needed counseling but the Parkers pretended there was no problem."

Lance pulled another bale of hay closer and sat on it. "How do you know all this?" He turned to Raul. "Did Marybeth talk to you about it?"

"No, she didn't." Raul sighed. "She told me only that it was all Faith's fault. How come she told you, Tristan?"

"She is my employee, remember. Besides, we have always had an easy relationship, Marybeth and I."

"You have been in love with her…" Raul said accusingly, half rising, before being stopped by Lance.

"Think man. Marybeth talked to Tristan because she perceived no threat in him. He talked to her like he does to one of his wounded animals."

"Thank you, Lance. It's true," Tristan remarked, thinking Raul must be truly delusional if he thought Tristan could look at Marybeth with any other feeling that friendship when he had Eleanor, who was a goddess on earth. How could Tristan love anyone else? "The reason why I know a little more about Marybeth is because lately she was pestered by an unsavory character, named Jody Coates."

"And you didn't tell me…" Raul asked with indignation.

"I couldn't. Marybeth told me all this in strict confidence. I promised not to tell a soul. Besides I called the police and Coates is in jail. He tried to poison my animals."

"Did Marybeth know him from before?" Lance asked.

"Yes, she met him when she was fifteen or sixteen. She was lonely and he charmed her by being nice," Tristan filled in, wondering how much Raul knew of Marybeth's trouble. At this point he owed his brother the truth. "Did you know she had a child when she was in high school?" he asked gently.

"Yes, she told me. She gave him up for adoption and she said she had to be sure he was okay. That's why she couldn't commit to me. Now she said the adoptive mother died and she's going to marry the widowed father. How did she know the adoptive parents? Weren't these adoptions secret?"

Tristan patted him on the back. "This was a private adoption arranged by Marybeth's aunt. The parents promised to send her news and pictures about the boy every year, if she promised not to ever interfere in their life."

"And now, because the mother died, the adoptive father condescended to marry Marybeth, despite her scar, - his words," Raul said with indignation.

Tristan shook his head. "Another trouble Marybeth jumps into without thinking. It is never boding well for a marriage if one is agreeing to marry despite the other mentioning her flaws all the time. She will have to kowtow to him to please him. I know you'll be mad at me, Raul, but this is what I believe - most of the problems Marybeth has, are of her own making. She was unfortunate once to have that accident, but after that she ran from one trouble to another, from one wrong decision to another."

Raul covered his face with his hands. "I love her. What am I going to do now, without her?"

Lance touched his arm. "Let her go, brother. Go on with your life."

Laughter could be heard outside the barn and Annie and Eleanor came in, singing a carol and swaying a bit. Too much cider, perhaps?

"Is this a private party in the new men's cave?" Annie asked smiling. "Can we join you?"

Eleanor, more perceptive, looked from one somber face to another. "We promise not to ask questions."

"We do?" Annie frowned.

"Not now at least," Eleanor amended.

"Ah, I see. The tree is decorated with as many ornaments that the branches could hold and Carmelita has prepared a special cake for the day after Thanksgiving. Let's go in," Annie said. "And enjoy the holidays."

"Enjoy," Raul contemplated the word morosely like if it were a dirty word.

Annie hooked his arm. "Yes enjoy and be happy for being all together, in good health, for having a large supportive family and love. Raul please smile and have a happier face if you don't want a full interrogation from your mother."

Later that night after a vigorous and satisfying

lovemaking, Eleanor kissed Tristan shoulder and nestled closer. "So what were you boys plotting in the barn?"

"Hmm?" No sense avoiding answering her. Besides everybody would find out soon. "Marybeth Parker left Raul to marry a guy from Nevada."

Eleanor stilled. "Are you serious? That girl is not right in her head."

"She had her reasons, but I think she jumped from a difficult situation into a potentially disastrous one," Tristan added.

"You're right. I think that Raul is mourning now the loss of his love, but he'll be better off in long run."

He kissed her deeply. "I love you Eleanor and I'm happy you're mine."

EPILOGUE

And the wedding was a tale of dreams to be remembered and shared with the children and grandchildren later on. The bride was like a fairy princess in her white lace gown, with her blond hair flowing down her back and a small bouquet of lilies-of-the-valley in her hand. The groom was dark and handsome in his tuxedo waiting for her in front of the makeshift altar near the Christmas tree.

It was one of the most gorgeous couples to be married, that people present had seen. The love that shone in their eyes when they looked at each other made them so perfect. A lot of people filled the large family room at the ranch house.

They partied and laughed and danced and enjoyed a memorable wedding celebration and Christmas holiday.

Outside, it was a cold night, dry, with clear sky, full of twinkling stars. Above the Laramie plains, the moon was smiling too, lighting the path of

the newlywed couple and wishing them a long, happy
life together.

* * *

The Maitland family saga continues

Book 1 – **Lost In Wyoming** – Lance's story

Book 2 – **Moon Over Laramie** – Tristan's story

Book 3 – **Christmas In Cheyenne** – Raul's story

To find out about new releases and about other books written by Vivian Sinclair visit her website at www.viviansinclairbooks.com

A Guest At The Ranch, western contemporary romance

Storm In A Glass Of Water, a small town story

A Walk In The Rain, women's fiction novel

Don't miss Book 3 of the Maitland Legacy, A Family Saga available from Amazon. Keep reading for an exclusive sneak peek of Raul and Faith's story.

Christmas In

Cheyenne

VIVIAN SINCLAIR

Chapter 1

It was Christmastime in Cheyenne. The streets were dry, but the cold air smelled of winter. A few snowflakes here and there started to fall from the heavy grey clouds. At 5pm the traditional Christmas parade started and people lined up along the streets to watch and cheer the one hundred thirty floats.

Raul made his way through the crowds, laden with packages, looking in the store windows. In the past, it had been only his mother and brother Lance he had to think about in terms of Christmas presents. Now, he had a large family, his father the Old Man Maitland, his two brothers Lance and Tristan and their wives, his nephew Zach, not to mention the ranch hands working for him who would receive a bonus, and also small personal gifts.

He inhaled deeply, breathing in the cold air. A snowflake melted on his tongue. Soon the ground would be covered by a thick white layer. A door opened right in front of him and raucous laughter could be heard from the inside, drowning out the Christmas carols from the loudspeakers. He looked at the sign above the door, 'Cody's Tavern'. Stuck to the window was today's special, meatloaf with mashed potatoes and gravy and apple pie. He realized that he was famished. He had skipped lunch and left the meeting early to finish shopping.

Raul entered the tavern where a bunch of rowdy cowboys were drinking beer at the bar, served by a tall, middle-aged barman, built heavy like a wrestler. For a second he considered going out in the street and looking for a better place to eat. But the flavors coming from the kitchen were appetizing and he was hungry.

He took a seat at a table near the window, facing the noisy cowboys. The paint was cracked and peeling in places on the walls, but the room was very clean and a piece of greenery with a red bow adorned every table. Christmas lights were twinkling in every window.

A slim, tall waitress was cleaning the nearby table. The jeans molded to her backside enticingly when she bent to wipe the table. Raul was a red-blooded male and appreciated the beauty of a woman's body. A few tendrils of dark hair had slipped from her ponytail, shading her face. She picked up the tray with dirty dishes and carried it to the kitchen. Raul looked out the window watching the people passing by.

"What can I get you today?" a sexy, low voice sounded in his ear interrupting his daydreaming.

Startled, he turned to look at her and had the shock of his life. "Faith?"

Cat-green eyes looked back at him mirroring the same surprise. "I... I..." she stuttered. He looked at the nametag pinned on her chest. It said, 'Cassie'. She watched him and considered pretending not to know him. Then, she shrugged. He was not important. "I go by Cassie now. It's my name, Cassandra Faith Parker."

Raul looked at her. Even though she was tired, with dark circles under her eyes, Faith Parker was a fine, beautiful woman. What was she doing waitressing in Cheyenne, instead of coming home where she'd be treated like a queen? Although the way she looked at him showed she was no less haughty. He shook his head. "What are you doing here, Faith? Last I heard you were a singer in New York City."

Her stubborn chin rose. "None of your business, Raul Escobar."

The correction came to his lips automatically. "I go by Maitland now. Raul Maitland is my legal name."

Faith frowned. Her sister wrote a while back, about an incredible story, how the nobody of a cowboy, son of the Mexican cook, came to be the owner of the large Maitland ranch and the best catch north of Laramie, not that he paid any special attention to any of the women condescending to flirt with him. There were 'sour grapes' in Dora's tone. Knowing Dora, Faith guessed she had tried to catch the elusive Raul herself and had been rebuffed. Faith was one of the few who knew why and that was

4

because she'd heard it by chance. Raul was in love with their youngest sister, Marybeth of the tragic fate.

Faith took her little notebook out. "What can I bring you?"

So, the conversation was closed. The secrets kept to oneself. Raul accepted that. "Today's special and the apple pie."

Faith bit her rosy lips and Raul's eyes shifted there. "The meatloaf is really good; it's made by our cook. The apple pie is so-so. I'd recommend the bread pudding instead."

"Who made the apple pie?"

An attractive blush colored her porcelain-white complexion. "I did," she confessed in a barely audible voice.

Raul laughed. "You Faith, cooked? I have to see it to believe it. Bring me a slice please."

"Don't say I didn't warn you," she said and left in a huff.

She was something, Raul thought. Down on

her luck, but still feisty and proud.

The food came soon and Raul dug into it con gusto. It was as good as promised. "Good," he said raising his eyes from the plate only to see Faith smiling. "What?" he asked, wiping his mouth with the napkin, wondering if he had gravy on his chin.

"I remember you always used to gulp down your food as if you had been starving for a long time," she explained. "I forgot your beer. I'll be back."

She went to ask the barman for a beer, when one of the cowboys ogling her tried to catch her arm. She eluded him. Then he placed his hand on her backside. Faith yelped and in one step Raul was there catching the offending hand.

"Now see here, who are you to…" the tipsy cowboy said.

Raul inclined his head to signal Faith to go to the kitchen, but the stubborn woman stood her ground. "I'm the man who will break your hand if you touch her again." With a sigh of disgust, he shoved the other man's hand back. The protests and mutterings of the others were stopped by the barman. "You heard him, boys. Calm down. And leave my help alone." They quieted, but the menacing glances they threw Raul's way predicted more trouble to come.

Faith came back with his beer and looked none too pleased. "You shouldn't have interfered. I can deal with the likes of them."

Raul wondered when had Faith learned to deal with rough people. She had been treated like a princess all her life. "You could say 'Thank you' just the same," he admonished her.

"Thank you. Are you happy now? Here is your bill." She placed a paper on the table.

"No way. I want my apple pie."

"Raul, I'll bring it to you, to go. Cody doesn't like it when I create animosity among customers and I really need this job until I find something better. Please go."

Yes, after all it was not his business what Faith was doing. He offered his help, and she rejected it. End of story. He placed several bills on the table and rose to go. She grabbed his arm. "Raul, ..." For a moment he thought she changed her mind, but she said, "...could you please not tell anybody you saw me here? I have my reasons..."

"Your reasons and your presence here are safe. You can keep your secrets." Taking his shopping bags, he left. He had enough of women and their secret reasons and their convoluted way of thinking. This was what Marybeth had said too. She loved him, but her reasons were more important and she had to go. Raul agreed with the first part, but he knew they could face any difficulty together. Only Marybeth didn't believe in 'together'.

Raul went back to his hotel and tried to put Faith out of his mind. But he had an uneasy feeling, a premonition, and after a couple of hours took his jacket and Stetson and went out again. The snowflakes were falling in earnest and a cold wind was biting. It was late and he knew that Faith was supposed to finish her shift. Cursing himself for not minding his business and for being a fool to interfere,

Raul approached the tavern. He raised his collar and pushed his Stetson low. After fifteen or twenty minutes, Faith, bundled in her parka with a green beret on her head and an assorted scarf around her neck came out of the tavern. She intended to cross the street when, from around the corner, a big, hulking shadow blocked her way.

"Pretty Cassie, we meet again. I know you and I will have much fun." He grabbed her arm and pulled her after him. "My truck is right here in the parking lot."

She protested and tried to pull her arm from his grasp but he was stronger. "Let go of me," she cried fighting him in earnest, but he was much stronger. Raul caught up with them near the truck and catching the man's wrist applied pressure until he released Faith.

"Do you remember what I told you? I can easily snap your wrist," Raul said and in a quick movement produced his ever present knife. "Or maybe I should cut you so that you will not forget."

The other one was a big bully, frightened when threatened. "I will not forget. I promise. You can have her. She's not worth fighting over." Opening the truck door he climbed in and sped away in a screech of tires.

Raul turned to Faith. "Well, I suppose you'll say again that I should not have interfered and I'll agree with you." When she did not give him one of her saucy replies, he looked more closely. Her pretty green eyes were wide with fright and she was trembling. "Faith, come here." He opened his arms wide and she nestled there crying softly. Faith looked to be at the end of her rope, like a person who had been hit by life one too many times.

How long they stayed there, in the parking lot, under the eerie light of the lamppost with the snow swirling around them, Raul could not say. After a while he coaxed her to tell him where she lived and reluctantly, she told him. He knew she would not have told him, if she were not scared.

Faith lived quite close, in a room above a crafts store. "It belonged to the old woman who owned the store. The present owner doesn't live here and rented it to me cheap. It's convenient, close to downtown. I don't have a car," she whispered.

Not having a car in Wyoming was tantamount to not have a camel in the middle of the desert. You could not survive. What was going on? Again and again Raul tried to tell himself he should see her home safely and leave. Not his problem. Only it seemed, like his brother Tristan, he was a sucker for lost strays.

"What's going on here, Faith?" he asked when they were seated on the couch that was probably used also as a bed for her, in the minuscule room. "Why are you here in this dump of a place, working in a tavern, instead of singing in New York City or going home to your parents? Tell me it's not my business again. I agree, but I had to ask."

She looked for a moment her mutinous self again, but then her face crumpled. "I can't do either, you see. My parents wanted me to marry Tom because he was wealthy and could take care of me, they said. I don't want anybody to take care of me. I wanted to go to New York City and be a singer on Broadway. I wanted to be a star. Two years ago when I left home my parents were so upset, they didn't want to hear from me. They said I burned my bridges never to return. Dora was the only one who wrote to me, in secret probably." She sniffed, looking at him with her beautiful green eyes, moist with tears.

"Parents say stupid things like that in the heat of the moment and then they regret it. Remember Maitland chased Lance away from home at eighteen. Probably he was sorry soon after, but the words had been said and Lance didn't come back."

"In my case they meant it. Every word. I think in an old-fashioned way they considered my being a singer a disgraceful profession and New York City a place of vice and sin. I don't know."

She brought two mismatched mugs with steaming tea from the tiny alcove that served as a kitchen. Raul accepted his, and wrapped his hands around it to warm them. "What about New York City? Was it not everything you had hoped?" he asked.

"Oh yes, it was. It was splendid and I was prepared to persevere, audition, accept rejection, and try again. Until one day when I had my big break. A director took a chance on me and gave me an important part in a new musical." She looked down into her mug. "I don't know if I should tell you this."

"You don't have to if you don't want to," Raul said smiling at her warmly. With a will of its own his hand rose and touched her cheek.

She closed her eyes and like a kitten rubbed her cheek onto his palm. "I want to but I am ashamed and frankly I don't understand myself what happened. But happened it did. My debut was successful. I was applauded by the public and lauded as an upcoming young star by the press. I was courted by agents who wanted to represent me. After ten great performances, in one of the shows, I started to sing a well-known melody, when a person in the front row had a burst of laughter and then coughed to cover it. I was startled and when I tried to continue

13

singing I could not. I panicked and tried again, only to croak like a frog. Desperate, I recited the words without singing. After that, every time I was on stage I panicked and could not sing. I was replaced by the understudy and my career was dead."

"It is called stage fright and all the great singers had it. They say Barbra Streisand was notorious for it. You didn't audition again?"

"Once. I started singing beautifully, but when the director asked me to go onstage and perform with a singing partner, I could not. I knew then it was the end of my career on Broadway."

37232776R00168

Made in the USA
Lexington, KY
23 April 2019